Too Precious to Lose

"We must act out our parts," said the *Marquis*, "and be careful not to forget them."

Norina looked up at him in amazement, then realized he was about to kiss her.

His lips had almost touched hers when she cried, *"Non! Non!"*

She was breathing quickly and was not certain what she should do.

Then the *Marquis* said quietly, "I thought you had agreed to play the part I have assigned to you."

"But... we were only... pretending!" Norina managed to gasp....

A Camfield Novel of Love
by Barbara Cartland

"Barbara Cartland's novels are all distinguished by their intelligence, good sense, and good nature...."
—ROMANTIC TIMES

"Who could give better advice on how to keep your romance going strong than the world's most famous romance novelist, Barbara Cartland?"
—THE STAR

Dearest Reader,

Camfield Novels of Love mark a very exciting era of my books with Jove. They have already published nearly two hundred of my titles since they became my first publisher in America, and now all my original paperback romances in the future will be published exclusively by them.

As you already know, Camfield Place in Hertfordshire is my home, which originally existed in 1275, but was rebuilt in 1867 by the grandfather of Beatrix Potter.

It was here in this lovely house, with the best view in the county, that she wrote *The Tale of Peter Rabbit*. Mr. McGregor's garden is exactly as she described it. The door in the wall that the fat little rabbit could not squeeze underneath and the goldfish pool where the white cat sat twitching its tail are still there.

I had Camfield Place blessed when I came here in 1950 and was so happy with my husband until he died, and now with my children and grandchildren, that I know the atmosphere is filled with love and we have all been very lucky.

It is easy here to write of love and I know you will enjoy the Camfield Novels of Love. Their plots are definitely exciting and the covers very romantic. They come to you, like all my books, with love.

Bless you,

Barbara Cartland

CAMFIELD NOVELS OF LOVE
by Barbara Cartland

Other Books by Barbara Cartland

A NEW CAMFIELD NOVEL OF LOVE BY

BARBARA CARTLAND

Too Precious to Lose

JOVE BOOKS, NEW YORK

TOO PRECIOUS TO LOSE

A Jove Book / published by arrangement with
the author

PRINTING HISTORY
Jove edition / May 1991

ISBN: 0-515-10574-0

Jove Books are published by The Berkley Publishing Group,
200 Madison Avenue, New York, New York 10016.
The name ''JOVE'' and the ''J'' logo
are trademarks belonging to Jove Publications, Inc.

PRINTED IN THE UNITED STATES OF AMERICA

10 9 8 7 6 5 4 3 2 1

Author's Note

THE discovery of the South of France as a resort for the British and which made it eventually the Playground of Europe in the Spring began at Cannes.

It was also said if Cannes was the creation of Lord Brougham, then Nice was the discovery of Smallett.

The Author of "Humphrey Clinker" found there was no English Colony there in 1763 and no English comforts.

But when he had written about it in his travels, the great humourist brought it to the notice of the sightseers.

Invalids also thought the mild weather of the Mediterranean would do them good.

That was the beginning, then gradually, year by year, Royal personages like the Duke of York spent the Winter there.

A few years later his brother, the Duke of Gloucester, stayed a few months at a Villa on the other side of the Paglione.

The Royal Dukes having led the way, English aristocrats began to make their own discoveries along the coast.

Beautiful Villas enclosing their own little Eden of semi-tropical vegetation began to appear on the hills.

Numberless paths led into lovely dells bright with wild flowers.

Beyond Villefranche, the beautiful village of Beaulieu, situated in one of the most sheltered rocks in the Riviera, drew visitors like a magnet.

The Marquess of Salisbury built a large pink Villa up above it with magnificent views of the Mediterranean.

To-day it is difficult to find a place that has not been built on.

But the Villa I describe at Cap d'Estel was actually built at the beginning of the century as a private house.

It has a small "Cap" of its own with the road high above it, and it is on the sea side of the railway.

It has a charm and a mystique all its own.

Although it is now an Hôtel, what I describe in this novel could easily have happened in the Villa in the past.

Nowadays it is more fashionable to go to the South of France in the Summer, where there are sun-bathers and sea-bathers on every rock.

But they cannot spoil the beauty and charm it had at the end of the century.

Then the wealthy aristocrats from all countries, including Russia, flocked either to Monte Carlo, Nice, or Cannes for the sun, and, of course, the irresistible excitement of gambling.

Too Precious to Lose

chapter one

1896

NORINA turned round when she heard a knock on the door.

"Come in," she said.

The door opened and a footman appeared carrying a tray.

He did not say anything, but thumped it down on the table and walked out of the room.

She gave a little sigh. Her mother would never have allowed anyone to be served in such a manner or by so surly a servant.

Her stepmother chose footmen by their appearance and had filled the house with servants Norina had never seen before. They were obviously not impressed that she was Lord Sedgewyn's daughter.

It would have been unheard of in the past for her to eat in her bedroom instead of one of the other rooms downstairs, even if she had not been allowed into the Dining-Room.

It was her stepmother who, whenever she could,

barred her now from attending the dinner-parties frequently given at the house.

Norina knew it was because of her appearance.

"There is nothing I can do about it," she said to herself when she looked at her reflection in the mirror.

It was because she was so lovely that from the moment her stepmother set eyes on her, she hated her. It was with a ferociousness which vibrated, Norina thought, across a room.

She was even conscious of it behind locked doors.

When her mother had died two years before, her father had been distraught.

Lord Sedgewyn had adored his wife. She was a sweet, gentle, loving person who wanted everybody around her to be happy.

At sixteen it was very difficult for Norina to know what to do about her father or how to comfort him.

They lived in the country, and he therefore went off by himself on long rides—only to return more despondent and depressed than he had been when he left.

Finally, as if he could bear the house no longer without his wife, he decided he would go to London.

He actually also had an appointment with his Solicitors to discuss the money his wife had left. He told Norina he would be back in two days.

To her surprise, the two days had lengthened into two months, and she had been getting very worried about him when finally he reappeared.

He certainly seemed more cheerful than he had been before.

At the same time, she knew that he shuddered every time he passed his wife's bedroom.

But it was less than a week before he said he had once more to go to London.

She realised later that because she was so young, she had never anticipated for one moment that her father would marry again.

But, five months after her mother's Funeral, he told her that he had asked a very attractive woman to take her mother's place.

Norina could hardly believe what she was hearing. Yet, because her father seemed happier, or, rather, less miserable, she said as little as possible.

She hoped that he would find some happiness with his new wife.

Violet Meredith, for that was her name, had been married before.

Her husband, Norina gathered, had left her very little money. She had appealed to her father in a bewildered fashion to help her understand her finances.

When Lord Sedgewyn's six months of mourning was over, he married Violet Meredith. It was then Norina realised for the first time that a disaster had happened to her.

Her father was married very quietly.

He went on a honeymoon with his new wife, then brought her down to Sedgewyn Hall to meet her stepdaughter.

Norina thought it would be impossible for her ever to forget the expression she saw in her stepmother's eyes, nor to misunderstand the vibrations of loathing that came towards her.

The new Lady Sedgewyn was, however, too clever to be anything but charming. She told her husband how delightful she found his daughter.

"What a pretty child!" she said in a cooing voice, "but, of course, dearest, how could you, being so handsome, have a child who was not in a small way a mirror of yourself?"

It was obvious to Norina that her father was delighted at the compliments his new wife paid him. He was also obsessed by her.

She was perceptive enough to realise that what he felt for Violet was not the love he had given her mother.

She attracted him physically.

She made him feel strong and masculine by her flattery and the caressing manner in which she always spoke to him.

"How can you be so wonderful!" she would exclaim twenty times a day.

She never spoke to Norina without saying:

"Of course, as your clever and brilliant father said . . ."

Or:

"Are you not a lucky girl to have such a splendid and understanding father! I only wish mine had been the same."

Norina realised this was a clever act.

She always made herself out to have had a sad, deprived, and often cruel life until Lord Sedgewyn rescued her.

She soon learnt to doubt the truth of everything that Violet said. She was therefore quite certain that this was just an act.

What, however, was not was Violet's determination to isolate Norina as much as possible from her father.

She suggested she should be sent to a Finishing

School, but Lord Sedgewyn would not hear of it.

"I do not approve of these Schools where they teach girls a lot of new-fangled ideas, and I want Norina with me."

Because he was adamant, Violet gave in.

She arranged, however, that Norina had so many Governesses, Tutors, and extra lessons of every sort that there was little time for her to be with her father.

Actually, in a way, Norina thought that she benefitted by this. Her education was far more comprehensive than any other girl of her age was likely to have.

It was the tradition among the nobility that, while the sons went to Eton, then on to Oxford, the daughters were taught at home; usually it was by a Governess who often knew little more than they themselves knew.

Violet determined that Norina should always be occupied and therefore not an encumbrance to her.

She hardly had a moment to herself except when she was riding.

Fortunately, Violet was not a skilful horsewoman.

The only opportunity Norina had to be alone with her father was to ride with him before breakfast.

It was then he talked to her as he had in the old days when her mother was alive.

She knew, although he did not admit it in actual words, he still yearned for the woman he had loved so devotedly.

They had spent some months in the country when Violet had the clever idea that she wished to go to London.

She persuaded Lord Sedgewyn that he should open

his house in Park Street. It had been closed for years for the simple reason that he preferred the country and so did his first wife.

Norina was left at Sedgewyn Hall with Tutors and Music Teachers coming every day to give her lessons.

She also had an attendant Governess.

She had, too, a French Teacher and an Italian one, a Dancing Master and a retired Professor who taught her Literature.

Of all her lessons, Norina enjoyed the Literature lessons most.

The Professor was a very intelligent man, and she found him not only an expert in English Literature but also that of a great number of other countries. He had visited the majority of these at one time or another.

She was in a way happy even though she missed her father. She also found it difficult to adjust to her life without her mother.

A dozen times a day she found herself wishing she had asked her advice on one thing or another. She wanted, too, to tell her something that she found exciting.

It was actually her Governess who brought her education to an end.

Lord Sedgewyn came down to the country to discuss the Estate with his Manager, also, to Norina's delight, to be with her.

It was then Miss Graham, who had been with her since before her mother died, said to Lord Sedgewyn:

"I would like to speak to you, My Lord, about Norina."

He smiled.

"You are not going to tell me, Miss Graham, that

she has done something reprehensible or that she is not showing the promise that you expected of her?"

"On the contrary, My Lord," Miss Graham said, "I think I should tell you that Norina is now too old and too clever to require a Governess."

Lord Sedgewyn just stared at her while Miss Graham went on:

"I have enjoyed being with her, and in fact she is the most brilliant pupil I have ever had or ever imagined having, but quite frankly, it is time she grew up."

"What do you mean by that?" Lord Sedgewyn asked in a puzzled tone.

"Norina is eighteen years and seven months old but mentally very much in advance of any girl of her age."

Miss Graham lowered her voice before she said softly:

"I think if Norina's mother were alive, she would want her to appear in London as a *débutante* and meet young people of her own age rather than spend her time with 'old fogies' like me and her other Instructors."

Lord Sedgewyn looked at Miss Graham in consternation.

"I see I have been very remiss," he said. "I had actually forgotten Norina is growing up, and you are quite right, Miss Graham. She must come to London for the Season."

"I hoped that was what Your Lordship would say," Miss Graham answered.

Lord Sedgewyn had been very generous to her. She announced that she was going to take a long holiday before she considered taking another post.

When she left, all the other Tutors were dismissed. Lord Sedgewyn said firmly that Norina was to come to London.

At first she was excited by the idea.

But when she arrived at the house in Park Street, she realised how furious her stepmother was at what had happened.

She had not seen her father and Violet together for a long time, therefore she had not realised how completely his life had altered.

The house in London had been redecorated from top to toe and very extravagantly.

There was a mass of servants Norina had never seen before. Her stepmother entertained every day and every evening.

It was obvious, however, that Violet was determined to exclude Norina from any entertainment that took place in the house.

Lord Sedgewyn had arranged that his sister should present her at Court. She was married to the Earl of Winterton.

Through her aunt, Norina was invited to a number of Balls at which there were other *débutantes* like herself.

She could not help feeling rather old compared to the other girls. She therefore did not enjoy the parties as much as she had expected to do.

She also realised that her stepmother begrudged every penny that was spent on her clothes. It did not take Norina long to become suspicious.

She was finally convinced that Violet was not only spending her father's money in an extremely extravagant manner, but also collecting from him every penny she could.

Violet expostulated angrily about what was being spent on Norina. It was then she learnt that the money with which she had been so prodigal had mostly belonged to the first Lady Sedgewyn.

She came to Norina's bedroom, where she was reading. One look at her face told Norina that something was wrong.

She had not been given a Sitting-Room, but a fairly large bedroom. There were two armchairs and a table on which she could have her meals if she did not go down to the Dining-Room.

Violet crossed the room and, sitting down in one of the armchairs, she said:

"I want to talk to you, Norina."

"What about?" Norina asked.

"I have learnt from your father," Violet said in a hard voice, "that your mother was a wealthy woman. Is that true?"

Norina hesitated for a moment.

She wanted to say that she had no wish to discuss her mother or her affairs with Violet.

Then she thought it would be a mistake to be rude.

"If that is what Papa told you," she said, "then of course it is true."

"Are you telling me that when your father dies the money he has use of now will be yours?"

Norina had read her mother's Will and she knew this was so.

She hesitated before she replied:

"I am not quite certain what the arrangements are, but I am sure Papa will tell you if you ask him."

"Your father has told me, though in a somewhat garbled fashion," Violet said. "I just wanted it confirmed."

"Then there is really nothing I can say," Norina answered.

"I thought when I married your father," Violet said angrily, "that he was a very wealthy man."

"We have always been able to have anything we wanted, Stepmama," Norina said, "but perhaps you want different things from those Papa enjoyed before he married you."

"What I want," Violet replied, "is to make sure that I am not left penniless, as I was by my first husband, and I consider it right that your father should, when he dies, settle on me everything he possesses."

She looked at Norina in a hostile way before she added:

"But apparently at least three-quarters of what I thought he possessed belongs to you!"

Norina stiffened before she said:

"Papa is not yet fifty. I cannot imagine, Stepmama, why you should be worried about what happens when he dies."

"That is the kind of idiotic thing a young girl would say!" Violet replied. "But when you are older you will realise that you have to look after yourself and make sure that you are not left desolate, having given somebody the best years of your life!"

She snapped the words at Norina. Then she went from the room, slamming the door behind her.

Norina sighed and thought it was very much what she expected.

From the very first moment she had felt that Violet's protestations of love for her father were merely a way of getting what she wanted.

"Why, oh, why," she asked herself, "did Papa marry anyone who was so very different from Mama?"

There was no answer to this. She began to think it might be wise if she suggested going back to the country.

At the same time, she knew that her father wanted her to meet the people to whom her aunt introduced her.

The first two months of the Season passed quickly.

Norina then began to think they might all go back to the country.

At least she would then be able to ride with her father early in the morning, as she had before.

"I must suggest this to him," she told herself, "without Stepmama realising the idea comes from me."

She was, however, finding it very difficult to be alone with her father. Somehow Violet always prevented it.

What was more, Norina realised to her consternation that in the evening he was drinking a great deal more than he had ever done before.

She was quite sure, although she could not prove it, that this was part of Violet's doing.

When dinner was over, she knew it would be difficult to have a coherent conversation with him. She would often hear him stumbling along the passage when he went up to bed.

She knew how horrified her mother would have

been. She began to pray that somehow she could rescue him from Violet's clutches.

However, she knew despondently it was something
Violet would never allow her to do.

She put down her book and walked towards the
table on which her dinner-tray was waiting.

She thought if her father asked where she was, he
would undoubtedly be told "with friends."

Even if she tried to see him later, it would be impossible. Violet's friends were mostly middle-aged
men who drank heavily and would stay until the early
hours of the morning.

Then, also, it was unlikely her father would even
be aware that she was in the house.

Violet had made it quite clear that she did not want
her downstairs to-night.

"Have you not an invitation for this evening?" she
asked. She spoke in the harsh voice she always used
to Norina unless her father was there.

"No, it is Monday, Stepmama, and there are seldom Balls on Monday."

"Well, I am having a dinner-party, and if you are
present, there will be more women than men."

"Then of course I will have my food upstairs,"
Norina said.

It was easy to acquiesce politely. It was far worse
to be told rudely what she would do whether she liked
it or not.

Actually, she had no wish to be with Violet's
friends. They either paid her extravagant compliments, which infuriated her stepmother, or else ig-
nored her completely.

She thought they were the sort of men that her father

in the old days would have called "Bounders."

But he obviously accepted them now because his wife demanded it.

She looked at the tray which had been set down without the footman troubling to put a cloth on the table. Nor had he arranged the dishes that were on it.

There was a small soup tureen, a china plate which had a silver cover, and a glass bowl containing fruit salad.

There was a jug of water, a glass, and a piece of bread on a plate. It had a pat of butter beside it because there was no room for a butter-dish.

It was not the way anything would have been served, Norina thought, if the new servants had not taken a lead from her stepmother. They considered her of no importance.

She sat down at the table, and as she did so heard a plaintive "meow." She realised to her surprise that the kitchen cat must have followed the footman up-stairs.

It was a rather ugly ginger cat. It was kept below stairs to catch the mice, which always frightened the housemaids.

Now it meowed again, and Norina wondered if it was hungry.

She would not be surprised. The servants were so different from those her mother had employed. They would not be particularly interested in animals of any sort.

In the country there were dogs and cats at home and the servants had been as conscientious in looking after them as they were for themselves.

The cat rubbed itself against her leg, and she asked:

"Are you hungry?"

She took the lid off the small tureen of soup as she spoke. She poured it into the plate on which it stood.

It smelt quite edible, if not particularly exciting. She wondered what they were having downstairs in the Dining-Room.

She knew her stepmother took a great deal of trouble over the dinners she gave to her friends. She insisted on the best and most expensive food.

She also served superb wines which she coaxed her husband into buying.

The cat was meowing again plaintively. Norina lifted the silver cover from the plate and saw the reason.

Fish of some sort had been sent up to her. She thought as she looked at it that it did not look very appetising.

It also had a distinct smell which had attracted the cat.

She wondered whether she should give it a few spoonfuls on another plate.

Then she decided she was not hungry.

"I think your need is greater than mine!" she said with a smile. She put the plate down on the floor.

She then returned to the soup, finishing what was in the pot.

The fruit salad, which contained peaches and strawberries, was delicious.

She was sure it was not being served in the Dining-Room. If it were, there would be cream to go with it, and doubtless another pudding as well.

Norina ate the fruit with delight.

At the same time, she thought that if she were at

Sedgewyn, she would be able to pick the peaches herself in the greenhouse.

There would be figs ripening on the trees, as well as plums and nectarines.

When she put down her spoon she looked down to see how the cat had eaten the fish.

The plate was half-empty, but for the moment she could not see the cat.

Then she realised he was lying in front of the door as if he were trying to get out.

"Do you want to go back to the kitchen?" she asked.

Rising from the table, Norina walked towards him.

Only as she reached the animal did she think it was strange he should be lying on his side. As she looked at him she saw his eyes were shut.

A sudden thought struck her, and she bent down to touch him. Then she knew without doubt that he was dead.

For a moment she could hardly believe it.

Yet as she made an effort to revive him, she knew it was hopeless.

The cat was dead and half of what he had eaten was still on the plate by the table.

She picked it up, looked at it, and put it down on the tray.

She then faced the answer clearly and calmly—her stepmother was trying to kill her.

In fact, she would have died if she had not given the fish that had been sent up for her dinner to the cat.

At that moment Norina was not hysterical or even agitated.

She felt calm and rather cold. If the cat had not come up to her room, she herself would be lying either dead or dying on the floor.

When she was discovered, her stepmother would have some very reasonable explanation.

Also, doubtless, she would have a Doctor who obligingly would certify that she had died of a heart-attack.

It was how her mother had died. It would be quite easy to pretend that it was something she had inherited.

Norina went to the window. She stood looking out over the garden at the back of the house.

It was a garden shared by a number of houses in Park and South Streets, yet there was seldom anyone in it.

As a child, when she was troubled or unhappy, she would run into the woods for comfort. She thought now even by looking at the trees, the flowers, and the green lawn, they would give her the answer to her question.

"What shall I do?"

Everything looked very quiet and serene. Yet the houses on each side of the garden, like sentinels, were imprisoning what lay inside.

It was then Norina started to pray to her mother.

"Help me . . . Mama . . . help me! I do not want to die. If she . . . fails this time . . . Stepmama will . . . try again. She . . . hates me and . . . more than . . . anything . . . else she wants . . . your money!"

Norina had been told by the Solicitor that her father had the handling of her mother's money for his life-time.

If she was not there to inherit it, then it would belong to him, and Violet would be able to obtain it.

"Help me, Mama, help me! I cannot die in such a futile manner!"

She wondered whom she could tell.

If she went to her aunt, her story might not be believed. If she went to her father, Violet would make quite certain he would believe she was having hallucinations.

She could imagine all too clearly Violet saying in her plaintive voice:

"How can she believe anything so cruel and wicked of poor little me?"

It was the sort of act she could do so well. Naturally her father would have to comfort her.

It was then, almost like a light in the darkness, she remembered there was one person in the house she could confide in.

He was a servant who had been with her father and mother for over thirty years. Dawes was now her father's valet.

Coolly, not allowing herself to panic, she moved the ginger cat very carefully from the door. She placed him in a corner, where he could not be seen.

She carried her tray outside so the footman could collect it from the corridor without having to enter her room.

She wondered how she could speak to Dawes. It might be a mistake to send for him.

Glancing at the clock, she realised that because she had eaten quickly, the guests would still be in the Dining-Room.

Dawes would therefore not have gone to the Housekeeper's room for the meal the servants had when they had finished serving dinner.

She hurried to her father's room, praying she was right and Dawes would be there.

She opened the door, and to her relief, he was.

He was a man of over forty who had come to Sedgewyn House first as a knife boy. He had raised himself year by year until he eventually became valet to her father.

He travelled with Lord Sedgewyn wherever he went.

Norina had therefore seen very little of Dawes since her stepmother had insisted on going to London.

But she had known him when she was a child and her mother had trusted him. He had always been a very good servant in every way.

As she entered the room, he was collecting the clothes her father had worn during the day.

He looked up as she entered and said:

"Good-evening, Miss Norina! It is nice to see you lookin' so well!"

"I want your help," Norina said.

Dawes put down the coat he had over his arm.

"Just like old times, Miss Norina, you comin' to me with one request or another! I misses th' country, an' I knows 'is Lordship does, when 'e thinks about it."

"Please, Dawes, will you come with me? I have something to show you," Norina said.

Dawes put down the things he carried on his arm and walked towards her.

She hurried ahead of him, and when they reached her bedroom she opened the door.

Dawes followed her in.

She shut the door behind him, and to his surprise locked it.

Then she said:

"I said that I had something to show you."

She walked to where she had put the ginger cat in the corner. Dawes looked down at it in surprise.

"Why, it be Ginger!" he exclaimed. "What's 'e doin' up 'ere?"

"He followed the footman who came up with my dinner," Norina said, "and because I thought he was hungry, I gave him the fish to eat, and when he had eaten it . . . he died."

She spoke quietly. But she felt suddenly as she said the words that she might burst into tears.

Dawes stared at her in astonishment. Then he bent down to touch the ginger cat.

There was no doubt that the animal was stiffening.

"He ate th' fish, you say, Miss," he asked as if he were getting it straight in his mind, "which was intended for you?"

"It was . . . my dinner," Norina said, "and it was . . . poisoned!"

Dawes stood up. She knew by the expression on his face that he understood what she was telling him.

"You have to save me!" Norina said in a voice hardly above a whisper, "otherwise, if I stay here, I, too, will be dead!"

For a moment Dawes did not reply. Then he said:

"Do yer really mean that, Miss? I can't believe Her Ladyship would go so far!"

"She hates me, Dawes."

Dawes scratched his head.

"Her's jealous o' you, right enough. Women be all the same, an' yer've grown as pretty as yer mother, an' I can't say fairer than that!"

"It is not only my looks," Norina said. "It is the money Mama left me. She has only just learnt that if anything happened to Papa, it becomes mine."

Dawes's lips tightened. Norina guessed he was not going to contradict that statement.

"Yer'll 'ave to go to Her Ladyship yer aunt," he said.

"She will never believe me! You know she will never believe me, and my stepmother will insist that I come back. Next time there will not be a cat to save me."

"Then what do yer suggest, Miss Norina?" Dawes asked.

She could not bear to stand looking down at the ginger cat that lay at their feet. She walked towards the window.

After a moment's hesitation Dawes came and stood behind her.

"I shall have to disappear," Norina said finally as if she were speaking to herself.

"Yer can't go alone, Miss, not without a chaperone."

Norina had already thought of this, and she was silent until she said:

"Perhaps I could find something to do. I could be a Governess to small children."

There was silence while Dawes thought this over. Then he said:

"Yer be too young for that sort of job, Miss Norina, an' too pretty. Yer'd get into trouble, one way or another, then yer'd just have to come back.''

"There must be something I can do!'' Norina said.
"I have been well-educated, as you well know. And
I cannot stay here and wait for my stepmother to try
again.''

Dawes was scratching his head, then after a moment
he said:

"P'raps, Miss, while yer thinks it over, yer could
be a companion to an old lady. Some of 'em likes to
have a reader 'cause their eyes aren't strong enough
for them to read for themselves. And at least yer'd
be safe until we can think o' somewhere better.''

Norina clasped her hands together.

"You are right, Dawes! That is just the sort of
thing. I could keep in touch with you and you could
tell me what is happening to Papa. I am frightened
for him too!''

"Yer don't suppose His Lordship would believe
yer if yer tells him th' truth?''

Norina made a helpless little gesture with her hand.

"Would you have believed me if you had not seen
the cat?''

Dawes shook his head.

"I'd 'ave thought yer were a-dreamin', Miss Norina.''

"That is why you have to find me somewhere to
go . . . and quickly!''

She gave a little shudder before she said:

"I will not eat anything in this house unless somebody else has tasted it first.''

"Yer'll not go 'ungry as long as I'm alive,'' Dawes
said. "But I agrees with yer, Miss Norina, yer can't

21

stay here, but Gawd knows where we'll find anywhere else.''

"Surely there is a place where one engages companions and anyone else who is employed?''

" 'Course there be,'' Dawes agreed, ''and this lot, 'though some of 'em are a bit queer, all comes from Hunt's in Mount Street.''

"Then that is where I will go," Norina said.

"I thinks that'd be a mistake,'' Dawes said. ''I'll go for yer, Miss Norina, an' all yer 'ave to think of is a new name an' produce some references.''

"I can write those,'' Norina said, ''and sign Papa's name.''

"Then yer do that, Miss,'' Dawes said, ''an' I'll go to Hunt's first thing in t'mornin'.''

He paused before he added:

"Yer understands, Miss Norina, it might not be easy to find somethin' suitable right away. Yer might have t'wait, an' while yer're waitin', yer'll just 'ave to be careful.''

"I will not eat the food in this house,'' Norina said, ''unless you bring it to me.''

She looked at Dawes piteously before she asked:

"You do not imagine she will try to kill Papa too?''

"Not as long as yer're alive, Miss!'' Dawes answered.

Norina gave a sigh of relief.

"No, of course . . . I had forgotten that. I have to die first so that Papa gets my money. Then she will get it from him! Oh, Dawes, what would Mama say if she were alive?''

Now the tears ran down her cheeks.

"Now, don't yer fret yerself,'' Dawes said.

"Yer've been saved by the mercy of God from a woman as oughta hang by her neck until her's dead! Yer're alive, an' that's the way we're goin' t'keep yer, one way or another."

He spoke in such a determined tone that Norina smiled through her tears.

"Thank you, Dawes, thank you! I knew I could rely on you," she said, "and you know there is nobody else!"

chapter two

NORINA went down to breakfast when she heard her father passing her door.

She knew her stepmother would not be called until at least ten o'clock.

As she entered the Breakfast-Room her father looked round.

"Good-morning my dearest," he said. "I missed you last night."

"And I missed you, Papa," Norina replied.

"Your stepmother said you had a headache," he went on.

Norina did not reply.

She had no wish at the moment to make any trouble.

She thought it was the sort of thing Violet would say.

If she had told her father that she had been sent upstairs out of the way, he would have insisted that she come to the party.

Lord Sedgewyn was helping himself from the silver entree dishes on the sideboard.

Norina watched him carefully, determined to eat nothing he had not sampled first.

During the night she had thought over what Dawes had said. At least her father would be alive for as long as she was.

"I am not really being selfish in running away," she said to herself. "I am saving Papa's life as well as my own."

She was quite certain now that once Violet had got her money safely into her father's hands, he would have a mysterious accident or an illness from which he would never recover.

The whole idea made her shudder. But she was determined not to be frightened to the point where she could not think clearly.

She helped herself from the dishes which her father had already sampled. Then she sat down at the table next to him.

As she did so, she thought he was not looking as well as he used to.

There were dark lines under his eyes which she suspected were also slightly bloodshot. His voice was thicker and sounded older than it had been in the past.

She wondered if she told him the truth and begged him to go away with her whether he would do so.

Then she knew the whole story would sound to him far-fetched, over-dramatic, and theatrical. Her father, who was a very logical man, would not believe her.

He might, however, challenge his wife with the story.

'Then there would be an unpleasant row and I am sure that eventually she would kill me,' Norina thought, 'perhaps in an even more painful way than she planned last night.'

The poison must have been very strong. The ginger cat had died quickly and without making a sound.

Norina wondered from where her stepmother had obtained the poison.

Then deliberately, she forced herself to think of something else.

She talked to her father, who said he was going out for the rest of the day and would be in at dinner-time.

"I hope it will not be a late one," he said. "I find it very tiring when people stay until the early hours of the morning."

"It would be nice if we could have dinner together, Papa," Norina said.

He did not reply. She was sure it was because he did not wish to appear unappreciative of his wife.

Lord Sedgewyn ate his breakfast quickly, then looked at the clock on the mantelpiece.

"I must be going!" he said. "I have a meeting in half-an-hour with the Prime Minister."

"How exciting, Papa! I am sure you will enjoy it."

"I doubt it," her father replied. "Politicians invariably talk too much and for too long!"

They both laughed. As he rose from the table, Norina rose, too, and kissed him.

"I love you, Papa!" she said. "Always remember that I love you very much!"

"You are a good girl, Norina," he said, "and very like your mother."

He left the room hastily and Norina sat down at the table to finish her coffee.

She usually drank tea. Because her father had this

morning poured himself a cup of coffee, she had done the same.

When she knew he had left the house, she went upstairs.

She looked into his bedroom, but Dawes was not there, as she expected. She guessed that as soon as his Master had gone, he had hurried to Hunt's Agency in Mount Street.

She went to her own room, which had already been tidied, if somewhat perfunctorily, by the Housemaids.

Sitting at the small desk which stood in a corner, she wrote herself a reference. She thought it would be exactly what was wanted if Dawes found her a position as a Companion.

It was, however, difficult to say what she could do until she knew what situations were vacant.

All they had really decided last night was the name she would use.

"It be no use yer 'avin' a reference as being good wi' old people," Dawes had said, "if I finds ye somethin' in a Nursery with children."

"No, of course not," Norina agreed.

"I thinks for the moment," Dawes went on, "yer'll have t' take what's available. But yer can't stay here, an' that's a fact!"

"I agree with you," Norina said, "but, please, wherever I go to, make sure they take me at once."

"I'll do me best," Dawes had said. "Now then, what are yer goin' to call yerself?"

Norina hesitated and he said:

"It oughta be somethin' yer can't forget. I've always thought if yer're asked yer name suddenlike, yer tells the truth."

"Yes, I understand that," Norina said.

She hesitated, then she said:

"I know! Do you remember that Governess I had for a very short time who married the Under-Manager of Papa's Stables?"

"Aye, of course I does," Dawes replied. "A pretty thing, her was. I never imagined she'd settle down in t' country!"

"Well, her name was Wyndham," Norina said, "and I used to laugh and say we must be half-related to each other, and that is easy for me to remember."

"All right," Dawes said.

He stayed talking to her until he was sure all the staff would be having supper.

Then he wrapped the body of the ginger cat in some old dusters. He carried it downstairs to put it in the dustbin.

He also emptied away what was left of the fish on the plate. The footman had forgotten to collect the tray from outside Norina's bedroom door.

"Careless b'aint the word for these young men," Dawes said, "but 'Er Ladyship likes 'em to be tall an' 'andsome, and yer can't expect 'em t' have brains as well!"

Sitting at her desk, Norina tried to remember the references she had read in the past so far as her Governesses were concerned.

She knew, however, that both her father and her mother believed it was better to use their intuition than to rely on what her father scornfully called "bits of paper."

When Violet had first married her father and they

had gone to London, she had heard that they were continually changing the staff.

Butlers had succeeded one another so frequently that in the end her father had said:

"You had better leave the senior servants to me, Violet."

"Of course, if you want it," Violet had agreed sweetly, "you are so clever and so very perceptive. I am sure you will never make a mistake."

Her father had therefore chosen the Butler who was with them now. He had proved to be considerably better than his predecessors.

Norina had the idea that it was Dawes her father had sent to Hunt's to make the preliminary enquiries.

She put down her pen and looked out of the window.

"Please, Mama, let him find me somewhere I can go," she prayed. "How can I stay here not daring to eat anything in case it is poisoned and wondering all the time what other means she will use to try to dispose of me?"

It was a prayer which came from her heart.

Then, because she was frightened, she walked across the room. She picked up the miniature of her mother which she always had with her.

She prayed that wherever she was, her mother would be thinking of her and loving her.

Then like a child she repeated over and over:

"Help . . . me, Mama . . . help me."

* * *

Norina had been right in thinking that Dawes had left the house.

He had gone out of the back door at the same time as his Master was leaving by the front.

It was only a short walk to Mount Street. He walked there so quickly that he was breathless when he arrived.

Hunt's Bureau was on the First Floor, and he climbed up the stairs followed by a frightened-looking girl. She had obviously just come to London from the country to try to "better herself."

The Domestic Bureau consisted of a long room. Prospective servants sat on hard benches just inside the door.

At the far end there was a high desk which was occupied by Mrs. Hunt.

Beyond that was a small room where a would-be employer could interview a servant without being overheard.

Beside Mrs. Hunt's desk, which was large and awe-inspiring, was a smaller one. This was occupied by her friend, who acted as her Secretary.

Mrs. Hunt did not look up as Dawes walked directly across the room to the desk.

Only as he stopped in front of her did she close the ledger in which she was writing.

"Why, it's you, Mr. Dawes!" she exclaimed in surprise.

Dawes politely removed his bowler hat as he said:

"Nice t' see you, Mrs. Hunt, and lookin' as bloomin' as ever!"

Mrs. Hunt, who was approaching sixty, simpered girlishly at him.

"Now, what can I do for you?" she asked. "Don't tell me that last Butler's got the sack, 'cause I won't believe it!"

"No, he be all right," Dawes replied.

"Well, that's a relief, at any rate!" Mrs. Hunt said. "I managed to place the last man Her Ladyship said was no good and the Duke of Hastings ain't found nothin' wrong with him!" She spoke aggressively.

She disliked the senior servants she placed in good positions having to return, especially if they were told they were "not up in their duties."

"Now, what I've come to see ye about," Dawes said, coming to the point, "is a young lady who be a distant relative of His Lordship, an' has asked me to help her find a position as a Companion."

"What would she want with that kind of job if she's a Lady in th' real sense of the word?" Mrs. Hunt asked.

"She's certainly that!" Dawes replied. "I gives you me word on it!"

"The only difficulty is," Mrs. Hunt said, considering it slowly, "that we've no one on our books at the moment looking for a Companion, but there's sure to be one in a week or so's time."

Dawes was disappointed.

"It's like this, Mrs. Hunt," he said confidentially, "the young Lady, an' ever so nice she be, is in straitened circumstances an' can't wait."

Mrs. Hunt put up her hands.

"What can I do?"

"What else you got?" Dawes asked.

At that moment Miss Ackroyd, Mrs. Hunt's assistant, rose to her feet and whispered in her friend's ear.

"I think I might be able to help," Mrs. Hunt said to Dawes.

She looked at him for a moment before she went on:

"Edith has just reminded me that we've got one applicant on our books who wants a Secretary as speaks fluent French, but he's asked for a man."

"Fluent French?" Dawes exclaimed. "Well, the Lady as I'm speaking of speaks several o' them foreign languages, 'though I could never get the hang of them meself."

"I have had only one man apply for the post," Mrs. Hunt said, "and he came back within the hour, saying as how his French weren't good enough."

She hesitated before she went on:

"The Gentleman as requires a Secretary is, as I understand it, elderly and blind and therefore the young woman would not care for a place like that, even if he would consider her."

Dawes was thinking quickly and he said:

"P'raps I've misled you. I said as 'ow the lady in question were young, which was somewhat of a figure of speech."

"You mean she's much older?" Mrs. Hunt enquired sharply.

"She be young in heart, Mrs. Hunt," Dawes said, "just like yourself. No one would call you old!"

"Oh, go on with you, Mr. Dawes! You're a flatterer—that's what you are!"

"As it 'appens," Dawes said, "I think the Lady what I'm concerned with be just the right person for an old gentleman as can't see, but is acute of hearing when it comes to French.''

''The servant as come here and is French was very insistent that he required a man.''

''Well, give him a chance to say 'no,' '' Dawes pleaded.

''He'll say it sharp enough,'' Mrs. Hunt retorted. ''The man I sent him yesterday come back like a dog with his tail between his legs!''

''Well, I promise you,'' Dawes said, ''and I swears as I'm speakin' the truth, that the Lady speaks French like a 'Froggy'!''

Mrs. Hunt laughed.

''All right, Mr. Dawes, you win, but if she comes back in tears, don't blame me!''

''I won't,'' Dawes promised.

''Just give me her name,'' Mrs. Hunt said, ''and I'll make out a card for her to present at the door, an' if the gentleman won't see her, you can only blame yourself!''

''I've taken some hard knocks in my life,'' Dawes said jovially.

''I'll bet you have!'' Mrs. Hunt said meaningfully. ''And softer ones too!''

They both laughed.

Mrs. Hunt picked up her white quill pen.

''Now, what's this Lady's name?''

''I thinks I forgot to tell you,'' Dawes said, ''but she be a widow.''

''A widow!'' Mrs. Hunt exclaimed. ''I thought you was talking about a young girl.''

''Her were a widow unexpectedlike,'' Dawes explained. ''Her 'usband had a nasty accident. Broke 'is neck out ridin', and left her without a penny to 'er name!''

"Poor woman, it must have been a shock!" Mrs. Hunt remarked.

"That it were," Dawes agreed, "and when her turns to me for 'elp, what could I do but try an' 'elp her?"

"You're too kind-hearted, Mr. Dawes—that's wot you are—always takin' other people's troubles on your shoulders!"

"I does what I can," Dawes said with a sigh.

"Well, what's her name?" Mrs. Hunt enquired.

"It's Mrs. Wyndham," Dawes answered, "spelt with a 'Y.'"

Mrs. Hunt wrote it down in a somewhat uneducated hand on a card. On it was already printed the name and address of the Bureau.

"My fee," she said, "is fifteen percent of the first three months' wages, which she might remind that Frenchie chap as came here in case he forgets."

"I'll ask Mrs. Wyndham to do that," Dawes said.

He put the card into his pocket and stretched out his hand across the desk.

"Thank yer for all yer help," he said. "I knew I could rely on yer."

"Don't you go 'counting your chickens before they're hatched!" Mrs. Hunt admonished him. "And if Mrs. Wyndham doesn't get the job, I'll try and find her something else, but it's not easy at this time of the year."

Dawes shook her warmly by the hand and also shook hands with Miss Ackroyd.

Then he walked jauntily back down the room.

While they had been talking, a number of servants, young and old, had occupied the benches.

* * *

Outside in the street Dawes hurried as quickly as he could back to Sedgewyn House.

He wanted to see Norina before Lady Sedgewyn was up and about. She would be doubtless expecting to hear that her stepdaughter had died during the night.

He slipped in by the door in the basement and hurried up the back stairs.

Knocking on Norina's door, he entered. She jumped up from the chair in which she was sitting.

"Oh, Dawes, you are back!" she cried. "Have you found a position for me?"

"I have, Miss Norina, but it's not quite what yer expected."

"I will go anywhere . . . do anything," Norina said, "even if it means scrubbing floors—rather than stay here."

"I understands 'ow yer feels, Miss Norina," Dawes said in a low voice.

He walked across to the window as he spoke. Norina, after one glance of surprise, realised why. He was moving as far away from the door as he could in case they were overheard.

As she joined him, he drew the card from his pocket and handed it to her.

"You *have* found me a place, Dawes!" she exclaimed.

Then she looked at the card, and before he could speak said:

"*Mrs*. Wyndham?"

"You're a widow, Miss Norina, for the simple reason you're goin' to be interviewed by an old gentleman who wants a Secretary as can speak good French."

"I can do that!" Norina exclaimed.

"He asked for a man!"

"A man!" Norina repeated in a different tone of voice. "Then . . . why should he take me?"

"There's no other person for the position at the moment," Dawes said, "an' the old gentleman refused to employ the man they sent him yesterday 'cause his French weren't no good."

"Well, at least I can speak fluent French!" Norina said. "*Mademoiselle,* if you remember, always said I spoke perfect Parisian French."

"I remembers that," Dawes agreed. "But, Miss Norina, you shouldn't stay alone with a gentleman!"

"What harm can it do if he is old and blind?" Norina laughed.

"It's something I can't allow," Dawes said firmly, "so that's why yer has to be a widow."

"But . . . what has happened to . . . my husband?"

"I tells Mrs. Hunt 'e had an accident out riding an' broke 'is neck."

Norina gave a little laugh.

"Oh, Dawes," she said admiringly, "how can you have thought of that on the spur of the moment?"

"Well, Miss Norina, it's like this," Dawes replied. "I knows it's goin' to be difficult to find yer anywhere to go 'cause yer're too young an' too pretty, an' even a blind old man'll 'ave friends as will talk."

Norina looked at him with wide eyes.

37

"Do you mean they would think it improper of him to have a young unmarried girl as his Secretary?"

"It's not exactly—improper for 'im, Miss!" Dawes said. "But they might treat yer in a way yer'd find—embarrassing."

Dawes was thinking slowly. He was obviously finding it difficult to answer Norina's question.

After a moment she said:

"I never thought a Companion would need a chaperone."

"There's Companions an' Companions!" Dawes said enigmatically. "As I tells yer from the beginning, Miss Norina, the only chance yer've got of being employed is if yer be an older woman."

"Then let us hope that the old gentleman will not object to a young widow," Norina said.

Then, as she looked up and saw the expression in Dawes's eyes, she said:

"You are thinking I must pretend to be old."

"Not *old*, Miss Norina," Dawes corrected her, "but not so young or so beautiful."

Norina made a helpless little gesture with her hands.

"Then . . . what can I do?"

"Well—I were a-thinkin' as I were comin' back to t' house," Dawes said, "that yer used to act them Plays with Miss Graham, an' very good yer were in them!"

Norina stared at him.

"Dawes, you are right!" she exclaimed. "If I have to be a Companion who is unhappy because she has lost her husband, then of course I can act the part. I can—of course I can!"

"That's wot I 'oped yer'd say."

Norina's eyes were shining as she looked at him.

She remembered how Miss Graham, who was a very good Teacher, had made her read all the Shakespearean Plays so that they could act out the parts.

At Christmas, to amuse her father and mother, they had staged a short Play, and it was sometimes written by Miss Graham herself.

Norina would be the lead. Some of the children in the neighbourhood would play the minor roles.

They would enact little comedies, sing and dance, while the servants in the house and on the Estate would be the audience.

Norina had loved every moment of it.

She thought now that she could easily play the part of a widow. No one would ever guess her real age or that she looked very different from how she appeared.

Dawes was watching her with his shrewd eyes.

"I shall need a black gown," Norina said aloud, "and of course a widow's hat with a veil, which is very concealing."

"I thinks too," Dawes added, "yer could wear some spectacles when there's anyone about."

"That is a sensible idea," Norina agreed. "But the first thing is to get my black gown and my widow's hat."

"If we goes out," Dawes said in a whisper, "before 'Er Ladyship finds you be alive, yer can say yer wanted something for your father, and I went with you to show you the shop he always patronises."

"Dawes, you are a genius!" Norina exclaimed.

She went hastily to the wardrobe. She picked up her hat and the little jacket that went over the gown she had on.

Her hand-bag was in a drawer, as were her gloves.

She started to leave the room. Then she remembered she had been writing her references at the desk in the corner.

She hurried to pick up the piece of paper on which she had scrawled a few words. She would have put it in the waste-paper basket but Dawes took it from her.

"Yer don't want t' leave anythin' incriminating about the place, Miss Norina!"

"No, you are right, Dawes," Norina agreed. "It was stupid of me not to think that anyone who was suspicious might look in the waste-paper basket."

"Yer've got to be watching every move yer make in the future," he warned.

He did not wait for Norina to reply, but opened the bedroom door cautiously.

There was nobody about, and they hurried down a side staircase.

As they reached the bottom of it, Dawes said in a whisper:

"Wait 'ere a moment, Miss Norina, I've got an idea!"

He left her. She wondered what he was planning, until a few seconds later he returned.

She saw then that in his hand he carried a key.

She knew it was the key which opened the door leading into the garden.

"Now, just yer walk across th' lawn," Dawes said, "open the gates at th' far end, which'll lead yer into the Mews. Go slow an' I'll be waiting for yer there."

Norina did not argue, but took the key from him and let herself out of the house.

She walked slowly under the trees, stopping occasionally apparently to admire the flowers in one of the beds.

If by any chance somebody was looking out of one of the windows, they would assume that she was just enjoying the morning air.

She reached the end of the garden. Quickly she let herself out by the door in the wall which led into the Mews.

She was half-afraid she had arrived there before Dawes. To her relief, he was already there and had a Hackney Carriage waiting.

As Norina got into it, he told the Cabbie to take them to a large Emporium in Oxford Street.

Norina had never been there herself. But she had seen it advertised in some of the Ladies' Magazines.

Only as they drove off did Dawes say:

"I've just thought, Miss Norina—I didn't remind you to bring any money with yer—so how will yer pay for anythin' yer buys?"

"I can write a cheque for the gown," Norina said, "and I have enough money in my purse to pay for the hat. It might seem a strange purchase if I paid for it by cheque."

Dawes looked relieved. Norina guessed that he had felt upset because he thought he had slipped up in his arrangements.

It made her realise that she would need a great deal of money if she was going to disappear for any length of time.

Fortunately on her eighteenth birthday her father had given her a cheque-book.

"One day, my darling," he had said, "your husband will handle your money, but I think it is a good idea, as it is yours, that you should be able to spend some of it without having always to ask someone's permission.''

''Yes, of course . . . thank you, Papa,'' Norina had said.

''You should know how to write a cheque,'' Lord Sedgewyn went on, ''and feel for the moment, at any rate, that you are independent even of me.''

Norina had thought that what he was really saying was that her stepmother would not be able to interfere in anything she spent.

To please him, however, she merely answered:

''I love having you to look after me, Papa. At the same time, I shall now be able to keep what presents I buy you at Christmas and birthdays a secret!''

Her father had laughed. Norina found he had put a thousand pounds in her name into the Bank.

In fact, she had spent very little of the money. When she had come to London, her father had insisted that he should pay for the clothes she was to wear as a *débutante*.

''It is a present to my beautiful daughter,'' he said.

Norina had been aware that her stepmother's lips had tightened. There was a flash of hatred in her eyes.

Violet had, however, praised her husband for his generosity.

''And I am very lucky to have such a lovely step-daughter to present to the Social World,'' she cooed.

Now Norina said beneath her breath:

''If she can act, so can I.''

The Emporium boasted it could provide everything a woman might ever want.

It produced a pretty black gown when Norina said she needed one for a Funeral.

She also bought a black coat to wear over it in case it was cold.

At the same time, she realised that black accentuated the whiteness of her skin, her hair which was "gold flecked with fire." This was how her father had once described her mother's hair.

When Norina went to the Hat Department, she explained that she was buying a hat for a friend who had been bereaved.

She tried on several.

The one she bought had a touch of white on the forehead. When the fine crepe veil was thrown back off her face, she looked a very young and very attractive widow.

Norina did not speak to Dawes while they were in the Department.

He kept very much in the background, and she heard him explaining to anybody who was interested that he was escorting the young Lady because her personal maid was indisposed.

Without him prompting her, Norina was wise enough to realise that she would need black stockings, black shoes, and black gloves.

On an impulse she also bought a black evening-gown which she saw hanging up as they passed through the Department.

Although it seemed unlikely, she thought it might be useful to have one.

She paid for everything by cheque with the exception of the hat.

Having left the shop, she said to Dawes once everything had been placed in the carriage beside her:

"I knew what you were thinking when I was trying on the black hats, and, while I can cover my hair in the daytime, I am wondering what I should do about it in the evening."

"I were a-wonderin' the same thing meself," Dawes admitted, "an' I thinks if yer're accepted for the job, I'll 'ave to get yer a wig."

Norina gave a little cry and clapped her hands.

"Dawes, you are brilliant! I never thought of it, but of course a wig is the perfect solution, and as I bought a lot of black ribbon, I can tie it where the wig joins my forehead."

"Yer'll still look young, Miss Norina," Dawes said, "so just yer remember to keep them spectacles on yer nose if there be anyone about, man or woman."

He sounded so worried that Norina answered:

"I will do everything you tell me, but I was thinking that one thing is very important. Once I have run away from home, I must be able to contact you."

Her voice trembled before she finished:

"I . . . might be in . . . difficulties . . . and not . . . know what to do."

"I was a-thinkin' the same thing meself, miss," Dawes said, "and it'll be quite easy. Yer can write to me care o' Mrs. Rolo, who be a relative of mine an' who I've just caught up with, so to speak, since I come to London."

"Oh, Dawes, that sounds an excellent idea! She need not know who I am, but you must make sure, if she did, she would not betray me."

"I'll tell her nothing," Dawes said. "At the same time, her be discretion itself—I promise yer that!"

Norina gave a little sigh.

"All I have to do now is to get the position, and you have to get me there."

"I was a-thinkin' about that while yer was tryin' on the clothes," Dawes said, "an' if it's all right, I'll take yer straight to Mrs. Rolo now. It's only round the corner in Shepherd Market where her's got a little shop."

Norina stared at him.

"You mean I can change there into the clothes I have just bought?"

"That's the idea," Dawes agreed, "then I can drive with yer to th' gentleman's house an' wait 'til yer comes out."

"Dawes, you are wonderful," Norina exclaimed.

*   *   *

Mrs. Rolo lived in a small house in Shepherd Market.

She was a large, rosy-cheeked woman who Norina thought should be in the country and not in London.

She greeted Dawes with enthusiasm and was very polite to Norina.

"Nice to meet you, Miss," she said. "I've been hearing about you from Andrew, and he tells me how pretty you are, but it were only half the truth!"

"Thank you," Norina said as she smiled, "and 'Andrew,' as you call him, has been very kind to me ever since I was a baby, so I think of him as one of the family."

"I've been telling him he should have a family of his own," Mrs. Rolo said, laughing, "but, there—

he always was one for the girls and won't settle down as he should!''

"What I says," Dawes retorted, "is 'there's safety in numbers,' an' Miss Norina knows as I always speaks t' truth."

When he explained that Norina wished to change her clothes, Mrs. Rolo took her upstairs.

The staircase was small and narrow. The bedroom, which Mrs. Rolo explained was there in case any of her relatives wished to stay, was tiny.

At the same time, it was spotlessly clean. Even the windows shone as if they were made of diamonds instead of glass.

Norina changed quickly. When she put on the widow's hat, she thought, as she had in the shop, that she looked too young to be a widow.

Perhaps, too, the Frenchman would think her too young to be a Secretary.

She looked at her reflection in the mirror.

Because he was blind, the gentleman would not realise that if she had been married, it could not have been for very long.

When she went downstairs, Dawes was waiting for her in the Parlour.

The front room was the shop, which contained a large amount of mysterious substances, some of which were herbs and elixirs that apparently Mrs. Rolo obtained from the country.

"Do I . . . look all right?" Norina asked anxiously.

"I thinks this be what yer need," Dawes answered.

He held out a pair of spectacles as he spoke, and Norina gave a little cry.

"How have you managed to buy these?"

"I found 'em in one o' the shops in the Market," he said. "They enlarge the sight a bit, but I thinks they'll make yer look older."

Norina placed them on her nose. When she looked at herself in the mirror, she laughed.

"Now I look like an owl," she said, "but certainly older."

Dawes was regarding her critically.

"Some of yer hair be showing," he said. "It'd be wiser if yer could tuck it away. I'll get yer a wig in a different colour from yer own."

"Yes, of course," Norina agreed.

Obediently she pulled her hat lower and tucked her hair underneath it.

Then she drew the veil forward so that it hung over the sides of her cheeks.

"That's better!" Dawes approved. "Now I'll get a carriage to set yer down at the corner of Hill Street so that yer'll be able ter walk up to th' house."

Norina understood. Anyone who was poor enough to need a job would hardly be so extravagant as to hire a Hackney Carriage.

Dawes was far more sensible in these matters than she was, she realized.

When they reached Hill Street the carriage drew up at the corner where it joined Berkeley Square. Dawes paid off the Cabbie.

Then he said:

"It be number forty-two, on this side of th' road, Miss Norina. I'll be waiting for yer when yer comes out."

Norina flashed him a smile, then hurried away.

She had no idea that Dawes, watching her as she

went, thought how elegant she looked in her black gown.

Her waist was very small. She walked with a grace and an eagerness that made her seem very young.

"I ought not ter be lettin' her do this," Dawes muttered beneath his breath, "but Gawd knows I can't think of any other way her'll be safe from that Devil!"

Norina walked up the steps to No. 42 and raised the silver knocker.

It made a rat-tat that was quite audible in the almost empty street.

Norina waited, feeling it was a long time before she heard footsteps inside.

Then the door opened.

chapter three

THE door was opened by an elderly man with white hair.

He looked at Norina questioningly. She took from her pocket the card which Dawes had given her and held it out to him.

"I have come from Hunt's Domestic Bureau," she said.

The man took the card and looked at it. Then, leaving Norina standing just inside the door, he walked across the hall.

He disappeared under the stairs and Norina heard him shout:

"Mr. Blanc! Mr. Blanc!"

She waited. The house appeared to be well-furnished and obviously belonged to somebody who had money.

A few seconds later a middle-aged man whom she guessed must be a senior Servant or Secretary came hurrying towards her.

He held the card from the Agency in his hand.

As he looked at her Norina thought he seemed somewhat surprised at her appearance.

Then he said:

"I tell . . . Agency . . . place . . . for man!"

His English was halting and he mispronounced some of the words.

On an impulse Norina replied in fluent French:

"It is impossible for the moment for them to find a male Secretary who is fluent in French. I have therefore come because, as you can hear, *Monsieur*, I speak French and I am an experienced Secretary."

The man stared at her in astonishment.

Then he said:

"You . . . wait—I speak—Master."

The servant closed the front-door. Although he did not ask her to do so, Norina sat down on a hall chair that was against the wall.

She sat upright, holding her hand-bag in her lap. She was praying in her heart that she would be accepted.

If not, Dawes would have to go back to the Bureau and she would be forced to return home. She would not dare to eat anything until Dawes found her somewhere to stay.

She had the feeling that it would be a mistake to ask Mrs. Rolo if she could occupy her spare bedroom.

Norina was sure she would agree.

At the same time, Shepherd Market was too near to her stepmother, and the servants would obviously shop there.

If she was seen, even her disguise might not be sufficient to prevent them from recognising her.

The Frenchman seemed to be away for a long time.

Then he came back to say:

"You . . . come!"

Norina felt her heart leap.

At least she had a chance if the old gentleman was prepared to see her.

The Frenchman walked ahead down a narrow passage and opened a door.

When Norina walked inside, she thought he had made a mistake. The room was dark, the curtains drawn over the windows, and the only light came from a fire burning in the grate.

Then she saw the man beckoning to her, indicating a chair just inside the door. She guessed it had been put there specially for her.

It was a hard upright chair, and she sat down on it.

As her eyes accustomed themselves to the gloom, she realised there was a man in the room. He was sitting in an armchair directly in front of the fire.

It meant that he had his back to her, and she could see only the top of his head.

The Frenchman walked to his side.

"*Madame est ici, Monsieur,*" he said in a low voice.

There was no reply, and he walked out of the room, shutting the door behind him.

Norina waited.

At last the man, who spoke in a deep voice, asked:

"*Vous parlez Français?*"

This she knew was her opportunity.

In her very best Parisian French she answered:

"*Mais oui, Monsieur,* I speak fluent French and

can write as easily as I speak. I am a proficient Secretary and am used to writing letters on behalf of whoever employs me.''

She paused for breath.

There was a silence until the man whom she could not see suddenly started to reply. He spoke with a rapidity which was quicker than anything Norina had ever heard before.

Her Teacher had warned her that the French spoke at a great speed. It was with a sense of relief that Norina realised she could understand every word.

The man in the armchair was asking her if she could translate political articles from a newspaper, if she understood the value of French money, and if she had travelled at all in France.

He used difficult phrases and ones that were not used in everyday conversation.

When finally he had finished, Norina answered him almost as quickly as he had spoken.

She told him once again how proficient she was and how easy it was for her to translate English into French, or French into English, whichever was required.

When she stopped speaking, there was silence.

Then the man sitting in front of the fire said:

''Your French is excellent, *Madame,* but I require a man.''

Norina gave a little gasp of sheer disappointment.

Then, because it was so important, she said pleadingly in a very different tone of voice:

''Please, *Monsieur,* please give . . . me a chance . . . I promise you I will do . . . everything that is . . . re-

quired of me, and it is very . . . important that I . . .
obtain a position . . . immediately."

There was a pause before the man asked:

"Why are you in such a hurry?"

"I have . . . nowhere to go and I have to . . . earn
my . . . living."

"You mean—you have no money?"

"Very little, *Monsieur,* but what is more important
is that I should find . . . somewhere to . . . stay."

She almost said "to hide," then checked herself at
the last minute.

There was what seemed to her to be a long silence.
Then he said:

"I must explain that I am asking for a Secretary
who is completely trustworthy and will not betray
anything that I say or do to anybody else."

"Of course, *Monsieur,* that is understood!"

"But—women talk, and you are a woman!"

"That is . . . something I cannot help, but I . . .
swear to . . . you that if you . . . employ me, I will
be . . . completely loyal and would never . . . do anything that might . . . hurt or . . . harm you in . . . any
way."

She did not quite know why she used those words.
She felt perceptively that they were somehow appro-
priate.

Again there was a long pause before the man said:

"How can I be sure that I can trust you? Because
I am blind, you will have to read my letters, however
private and personal they may be."

"That, of course, I understand, and if you . . . employed a man you would . . . expect him to behave . . .
like a Gentleman. I can only . . . promise you, *Mon-*

sieur, that I will . . . behave like . . . a Lady.''

"That is what I am afraid of!''

There was, however, a hint of laughter in the man's voice. It struck Norina that he did not sound as old as she had been led to believe.

Because she felt that she was losing rather than gaining ground, she said:

"I do not know . . . how I can promise you that . . . everything I do for you will remain . . . a secret, except if I say that I vow it on . . . everything I hold . . . sacred.''

"Are you a Catholic?'' the man asked.

Norina hesitated, then she told the truth.

"I was baptised a Catholic because my mother was one, but because she adored my father and wanted always to be with him, they worshipped together in the village Church, and I with them.''

"But she had you baptised in her own faith!''

"Yes, *Monsieur,* but I believe God hears our prayers whatever . . . label is put on us . . . so it is not . . . important.''

"That is a very interesting explanation!''

Again there was a hint of laughter in the man's voice.

"Please . . . please, *Monsieur,* give me . . . a chance!'' Norina pleaded.

She had a sudden fear that after all they had said, he would tell her to go away. She would then have to face the horror of what was awaiting her in her father's house.

It seemed as if a century passed before the man in front of the fire said slowly:

"If I answer that question in the affirmative, how soon could you come to me?"

"Do you . . . mean that . . . do you . . . really mean . . . it?" Norina asked.

Now there was a lilt in her voice that had not been there before.

Then, as she realised she had not answered his question, she replied:

"I can come . . . this afternoon, I just have to . . . collect my luggage."

"Very well, *Madame*, I will expect you in two or three hours' time."

"Thank you, oh, thank you, *Monsieur*, you are very kind! I can only say . . . again that I will never let . . . you down and I am grateful . . . more grateful than I can put . . . into words."

She rose to her feet as she spoke. Before she could step forward to shake his hand, he must have pressed a bell.

The door opened and Jean came quickly into the room.

"*Madame* is fetching her luggage," the man in the chair said, "and will join us in a few hours."

Jean opened the door wider and waited for Norina to leave the room.

She looked back at the top of the head she could just see above the armchair.

"*Merci, Monsieur, merci beaucoup!*" she said, and walked out into the hall.

She followed Jean and he opened the front-door for her.

"I am very glad that I am coming back here!" she said in French.

"*Moi aussi, Madame,*" he replied.

He bowed as she went down the steps. Then she heard the door shut behind her.

She hurried down the street, knowing that Dawes would join her.

It would, however, be a mistake for Jean to realise a man had been outside waiting for her.

Dawes did not come to her side until she was almost in Berkeley Square.

"Yer've got the position, Miss Norina?" he asked.

"I have got it, Dawes! It was difficult, and I thought at first he would send me away because I was a woman."

"That's good news, very good news!" Dawes exclaimed. "And when do you start?"

"As soon as I can collect my luggage."

As she spoke, Norina realised that that in itself was another problem.

"I've been thinkin' about that, Miss Norina," Dawes said. "I'll go back an' pack yer things an' bring 'em to yer at Mrs. Rolo's."

"But . . . supposing my stepmother sees you and asks questions?"

Dawes drew a watch from his breast-pocket and looked at it.

"It be after a quarter past noon," he said, "an' 'Er Ladyship's attendin' a large luncheon party. She'll be leavin' the house in a quarter-of-an-hour."

Norina gave a sigh of relief.

"Then you can pack everything for me, Dawes, and it had better be everything I possess. It would be a mistake to spend money unnecessarily."

Even as she spoke she gave a little cry.

"Money!" she exclaimed. "I must have some money with me! I have very little in my purse, having paid cash for my hat."

"I thinks o' that, Miss Norina," Dawes said, "and I suggests we go to th' Bank so's yer can cash a cheque. Yer've got yer cheque-book with yer?"

"It is in my hand-bag," Norina replied.

Dawes hailed a Hackney Carriage and they got into it.

He gave the name of Lord Sedgewyn's Bank to the cab-driver and told him it was in Mount Street.

As they drove along, Norina drew her cheque-book from her hand-bag.

"Perhaps," she said as she looked at it, "it would be a mistake for me to go inside the Bank. I have been there with Papa."

"I'll fetch out an ink-pot and pen for you, Miss Norina," Dawes said, "and say you've 'urt your foot an' it's painful to walk on."

Norina gave a little laugh.

"So many lies! I am sure you remember, as Nanny always said, 'one lie leads to another, and all lies lead to Hell!' "

"That's one place yer're ain't goin', not if I have anythin' t' do with it!" Dawes said stoutly.

When they reached the Bank there was no difficulty.

Dawes, as he said he would, fetched her pen and ink. Norina wrote out a cheque for three hundred pounds.

"It seems such a lot of money," she said, "but you never know, my stepmother might instruct the Bank to alert her if I go in for any more."

"Yer keep it well hidden," Dawes warned. "No

one will suspect a person who's earning her living to 'ave much money.''

As an afterthought he asked:

''Did th' Gentleman say 'ow much he was a-payin' yer?''

''No, and I did not think to ask him,'' Norina replied.

''I should 'ave reminded yer,'' Dawes said. ''To them as 'as to work, money's important.''

''I realise that,'' Norina said, ''but I have the feeling he will be generous.''

She did not say any more. Yet she felt Dawes was somewhat sceptical, as if he thought she was going to be cheated.

The Hackney Carriage took them back to Shepherd Market. Norina slipped quickly into Mrs. Rolo's house, hoping nobody noticed her.

Dawes kept the carriage and drove back to Park Street.

He was too sensible to drive up to the house, and got out at the corner.

Norina had given him the money with which to pay the cab-driver. When she had tried to give him something for himself, he refused.

''Yer'll need every penny yerself, Miss Norina,'' he said, ''an' don't go bein' too generous with it either. They'll expect a woman as is 'ard-up to count th' coppers.''

''Then that is what I will do, Dawes,'' Norina promised. ''But do not forget—if you ever need anything—you only have to ask me.''

She thought as she spoke that she would much rather Dawes had her money than her evil stepmother.

At the same time, it seemed horrible that any woman, or man for that matter, would be prepared to kill her just because they wanted her money.

She was touched to find that Mrs. Rolo had prepared an elaborate meal for her.

"How kind of you to take so much trouble!" she exclaimed.

She sat down in the small kitchen which shone as cleanly as the rest of the house.

"I enjoys having someone to cook for," Mrs. Rolo said, "and to tell the truth, Miss, I loves company. I misses me old man more'n I can possibly say!"

"When did he die?" Norina asked.

"Nigh on four year ago! I wept me eyes out every night 'til Andrew come along to cheer me up."

"It is good for him, now that he is in London so much with my father, to have you," Norina said.

"That's what he says," Mrs. Rolo agreed. "But he spends too much time with me, which is kind. I tells him there's plenty of young girls only too willing to 'step into my shoes.' "

"I am sure he would rather be with you," Norina said.

She enjoyed her luncheon.

When it was finished, Mrs. Rolo hurried into the shop. Norina sat waiting for Dawes to return.

When he did, she peeped out of the window. She saw that the Hackney Carriage in which he had arrived was filled with her luggage.

He must, she thought, have remembered everything she had brought with her from the country. This included two or three mauve gowns she had worn as half-mourning for her mother.

They at least might come in useful when she was working for the blind man. He would not be able to see what she was wearing.

"At the same time, I must be careful," she told herself.

As Dawes had said to her—servants talk.

He came into the kitchen and she exclaimed:

"I can see you must have remembered everything! How clever you are!"

"Just as I thinks, Miss Norina," Dawes said, " 'Er Ladyship had gone out, but it seems she's asked a lot of questions about yer and where yer was."

"What did she say?" Norina asked nervously.

"I thinks," Dawes answered, "although no one else realises it, her was very surprised to find yer weren't lyin' as dead as poor Ginger this mornin'!"

Norina shivered.

"Did she ask where I had gone?"

"Mr. Bolton tells her yer must 'ave slipped out after breakfast, as he didn't see yer leave the house. Then he says t' her:

" 'I 'spects as 'ow Miss Norina's gone to Her Ladyship. I knowed as how she were lunching with 'er to-day.' "

Norina put her fingers up to her lips.

"Oh, Dawes, I forgot! I was supposed to be lunching with my aunt, and of course I should have let her know."

"Yer leave things as they be," Dawes said. "Yer've got away, an' that's all that matters for the moment."

"Did they not think it strange that you were packing my luggage and taking it away with you?"

"I tells 'em yer was goin' to the country for a few days with some friends, an' yer asked me to pack yer clothes and convey them to Victoria Station."

"Oh, Dawes, did they believe that?"

" 'Course they does!" Dawes replied with a grin. "An' when I gets back I'll say as a servant I've never set me eyes on afore comes for yer luggage and I leaves it with 'im."

Norina laughed.

Dawes's tale was so evasive that it would be a long time before anybody realised she was nowhere to be found.

Yet he could not possibly be held responsible for her disappearance.

"You are very clever!" she enthused. "And you know how grateful I am."

"I don't know what yer'll think of this," Dawes said, holding out a paper bag as he spoke.

Before she opened it, Norina guessed what it contained.

It was quite a pretty wig of dark brown hair. It was obviously made to be worn on the stage and was curled and elegantly arranged with a chignon at the back.

Norina had taken off her widow's hat while she was having luncheon. Now, lifting up the wig, she ran to the mirror that hung on a wall.

It was a little tight, but it fitted her quite neatly.

If she arranged the black ribbon where the wig joined her forehead, no one would suspect for a moment that it was not her own hair.

It certainly made her look very different. She was sure that even her father would not recognise her if he saw her unexpectedly.

"It ain't bad!" Dawes said with satisfaction.

"It is beautiful, and I look different without being too ugly."

"Yer could never be that, Miss Norina," Dawes said loyally. "But yer don't look like yerself, an' that's a fact!"

Norina arranged her widow's hat on top of the wig, then put on the spectacles.

"The only thing I am afraid of," she said, "is being seen unexpectedly. If I suddenly appear looking like myself, I might be turned out of the house for being an impostor."

"Yer be very careful, Miss Norina!" Dawes warned in a serious voice. "And if yer in any trouble, yer come right back 'ere to me—d'yer understand?"

"Of course I understand, Dawes, and I will do exactly as you say, but I cannot see myself getting into any trouble of the sort of which you are so afraid."

Dawes shook his head.

"Yer can't trust them there Frenchies," he said. "If the old gentleman 'as a lot o' friends, yer keep outa sight. Remember, 'Er Ladyship will be lookin' for yer, an' careless words can cost a man 'is life!"

"Or a woman's," Norina said beneath her breath. Then with an effort she forced a smile to her lips.

"You have been so wonderful over this, Dawes," she said, "and one day I will be able to tell Papa how kind you have been to me. Promise you will tell me if anything happens to him? And, of course, warn me if my stepmother appears to be on my track?"

"Just yer let me know if yer 'as to move on, Miss

Norina. That French gentleman might wish to go 'ome.''

"I hope he does!" Norina replied. "I shall feel safe if I am far away in France."

"Wherever yer goes, yer write t' me 'ere,'' Dawes ordered. "I'll call round every day t' see if there's a word from yer.''

"Thank you for that, Dawes," Norina said. "There is nothing else I can say except 'Thank you' again and again!''

She put out her hand and Dawes shook it solemnly.

He opened the door for her. Quickly, so as not to draw attention to herself, she hurried into the carriage.

Dawes gave the Cabbie the address, and they drove off.

It took them only a very short time to reach the house in Hill Street.

Norina found she had quite a large sum to pay the cab-driver, but she knew, because Jean was listening as he carried in her luggage, it would appear that she had come a long distance.

"I am afraid I have quite a number of trunks with me,'' she said apologetically, "but I have come up from the country and brought everything I possess.''

Jean did not reply.

She thought he looked rather grumpy at having to take so many things upstairs. It involved a number of journeys for both him and the man-servant.

Her bedroom was large and comfortable.

Her trunks had been piled against one wall. She sat down in front of the mirror and very carefully removed her hat.

She also took off the small jacket that went with her gown.

Very neatly she arranged the black ribbon so that it concealed the edge of the wig at the hairline.

She felt she was looking at a stranger, but at the same time she looked older.

Just as she was wondering what she should do next, there was a knock on the door.

Quickly she put on her spectacles before she crossed the room to open it.

Jean was standing outside.

"The Master wishes to see you, *Madame*," he said in French.

It was an improvement on his very bad English, and Norina replied:

"I will come at once. If he requires me to write any letters for him, I am afraid I shall need ink and a pen, which I do not have with me."

"I will see to it, *Madame*," Jean replied.

She followed him down the stairs.

When he opened the door of the room she had been in before, she saw to her relief that the curtains were drawn back. The sunshine was shining through the windows.

The armchair in which the blind man had been sitting had now been moved from the front of the fireplace to the side.

For a moment Norina stood just inside the door, taking in her surroundings.

Now, for the first time, she was able to see the man who had employed her.

One quick glance told her that he was quite different from what she had expected.

His eyes were heavily bandaged, and she could not see above the end of his nose.

She realised, however, now that she could see his mouth and chin, that he was not, as she had understood, an old man.

She had seen the top of his head, but now she realised he had thick dark hair. It was brushed back from what, when it was not bandaged, should be a high forehead.

He was tall and certainly more broad-shouldered than she would have expected of a Frenchman.

He sat in his chair with his legs crossed. She had the impression that he was, in fact, slim and athletic.

Jean went out of the room, shutting the door. Feeling unexpectedly a little shy, Norina moved forward.

"So you have come back," the Frenchman said, "and bringing, I understand, a mountain of luggage with you!"

"I must apologise for having so much," Norina replied, "but you will understand, *Monsieur*, that I am at the moment travelling with everything I possess, until I find somewhere permanent to settle down."

"And you really think that will be with me?"

"I . . . I am hoping . . . so," she answered.

"I was thinking when you left," the Frenchman said, "that I had been somewhat remiss in not making it clear that if I find the right type of man to take your place, I shall ask you to leave."

Norina drew in her breath.

Then she said:

"I can only hope, and perhaps pray, that it will be a . . . long time before . . . he turns up like the proverbial 'bad penny.'"

She said the last words in English, and the Frenchman laughed.

There was a silence, and Norina wondered if she
could sit down.

Then he said:

"I have some work for you to do. Look on the
desk. You will find some letters there."

Norina walked to the desk which stood in front of
the window.

There was a pile of letters which she realised must
have accumulated while he had been blind.

She picked them up and went back to the fireplace.

"I have found them, *Monsieur,* and there are quite
a number."

"You will have to read them to me," the Frenchman said, "but do not bother with the bills, just the
invitations and the private letters."

Norina sat down in the chair opposite him, where
there was a small table beside her.

She quickly sorted out the bills and put them down
on it.

There were a number of envelopes she knew immediately contained invitations.

They looked like the ones she had opened for her
aunt. She even thought she recognised the hand-
writing on some of them.

She went back to the desk for a letter-opener. She
found it had a gold handle and was engraved with a
monogram.

Norina realised she did not yet know her employer's
name. She wondered if she should ask him what it
was.

Then she told herself she need open only one of the invitations to find it inside.

She slit open an envelope, then saw what she knew must be his name on top of the card:

Le Marquis de Carlamont

For a moment her eyes widened.

She had not expected her employer, who had taken her on in such an unusual manner, to be so distinguished or of such importance.

"There is an invitation here, *Monsieur,*" she said aloud, "from Lady Heatherton for dinner the day after tomorrow."

There was silence before the *Marquis* said:

"See what other invitations there are. I will tell you how to answer them."

Norina opened four more invitations.

Two were for dinner-parties, two were for Balls to which he was invited and asked to dine first.

She put them in a neat pile also on the side-table. Then she said:

"There are two letters here, *Monsieur,* and both appear to be in the same hand-writing."

She saw the *Marquis*'s lips tighten before he replied:

"Then, of course, as I cannot read them myself, you will have to read them for me."

The tone of his voice told Norina that he very much disliked anybody reading what had been written personally to him. There was, however, no alternative.

Norina opened the first letter, realising as she did so that it was scented with an exotic fragrance.

She started to read the first line, then paused to say a little nervously:

"This is a very private letter, *Monsieur*. It is written in English. Would you like me to read it in that language, or would you prefer it in French?"

For a moment the *Marquis* did not reply.

Then he said harshly:

"Read it as it was written to me!"

Norina felt she would have rather translated it into French. But she could only obey his orders and she read aloud:

My Dearest Adorable Alexus,

I cannot tell you how deeply distressed I am at what occurred last night. How could I have guessed for one moment that Hugo would come home unexpectedly and find you here?

He was very angry and told me he had taught you a lesson. I do not know what he meant, but if he has hurt you, I shall be very upset.

I love you—I love you, Alexus, and how could I have guessed when Hugo said he would not be back until the early hours that he would return so quickly?

I know it was wrong of me to deceive you into thinking he would be away all night, but I longed to see you. I wanted your kisses, your arms around me, and to know that you love me as I love you.

Oh, Alexus, I must see you again! I cannot live without you and I cannot bear to think that you might be angry with me.

Write to me and send the letter care of my

*maid, as you have done before, and remember,
I shall be waiting . . . waiting and counting the
hours until once again I can be in your arms.*

*Yours Adoringly,
Patsy.*

Norina finished reading the letter and looked across
at the *Marquis*.

She had been aware while she was reading that he
was very angry. She could feel the vibrations coming
from him were those of fury.

Because she felt embarrassed, she remained silent
as she replaced the letter in its envelope. Then she
opened the other one that had lain on her lap.

When she unfolded the letter, she knew she had
been right in thinking it came from the same person.

As the *Marquis* still did not speak, she said:

"Here is the . . . second of the . . . two letters."

She read aloud:

Beloved Alexus,

*Fantastic, wonderful news! Hugo is going to
the Doncaster Races to-morrow!*

*I have questioned the friends with whom he is
staying to make certain there is no mistake.*

*Oh, My Darling, this is my chance to see you
again! Come to me! Come to me!*

*I shall be waiting at the garden-door at ten
o'clock. I love you and I know I shall die if you
disappoint me!*

Patsy.

Norina's voice died away and she put the letter back in its envelope.

"That is all, *Monsieur*," she said.

"I can feel your condemnation without you expressing it!" the *Marquis* remarked.

"I . . . I am sorry, *Monsieur,* if . . . that is the . . . impression I have given . . . you," Norina replied.

"You sounded shocked and very disapproving," the *Marquis* remarked accusingly.

"But not . . . particularly . . . of you," Norina said impulsively.

"Then of whom?"

Norina thought it would be a mistake to answer the question. Yet just as she might have discussed the subject with her father, she said:

"I suppose I am . . . shocked that . . . any woman who is . . . married should be so . . . blatantly unfaithful to . . . her husband."

There was a twist to the *Marquis*'s lips as he said, and his voice was bitter:

"Then you must have been living in the country, for you obviously have little knowledge of London."

"It is not . . . the sort of . . . knowledge I wish to . . . acquire," Norina answered.

"I suppose by now you can understand what happened?" the *Marquis* said.

It was a question, and after a moment Norina replied:

"Did the . . . husband of the . . . Lady who has . . . written to you . . . hurt your eyes?"

She thought as she spoke she was being rather brave in asking such a question.

"He fired at me with a shot-gun," the *Marquis*

replied. "I was fortunate in that I was wearing an overcoat, which received the majority of the pellets, and my hat was also spattered with them. However, a number embedded themselves in the skin around my eyes and to save my sight the Doctors have insisted that I keep them bandaged for quite a long time."

Norina stared at him.

This was something she had never anticipated might be the reason for his blindness. In a voice he could hardly hear she said:

"He ... shot at you ... even though ... you were ... unarmed? I cannot believe ... anyone who was ... a Gentleman could ... do such a thing!"

"The man in question will tell you he is a Nobleman and therefore does not have to behave like a Gentleman!"

"I think it is ... utterly disgraceful!" Norina said. "And if it was ... known he would be ... turned out of his Club ... and no ... decent man would ... speak to ... him."

"I can see, *Madame,* you have an idealistic view of how English Gentlemen behave, but I am afraid when it comes to jealousy, they are as *gauche* as any *gamin* in the back-streets of Paris!"

Now the bitterness in the *Marquis*'s voice was unmistakable.

Norina clasped her hands together.

"But if the Oculist ... says you will ... get well, surely it is ... only a ... question of ... time?"

"Yes—time," the *Marquis* said, "but I have no intention of being laughed at and sneered at for trusting a woman who was quite obviously untrustworthy!"

71

"Then . . . what can you do?" Norina asked.

"I will leave to-morrow for Paris," the *Marquis* said. "Are you prepared to come with me?"

"Yes . . . yes . . . of course," Norina agreed.

"Then answer the invitations formally by saying:

"'*Le Marquis de Carlamont* thanks you for your kind invitation but has had unexpectedly to return to France, owing to the illness of one of his relatives.'"

"A-and the . . . letters?" Norina asked.

"Tear them up—throw them in the fire and let her wait!" the *Marquis* answered.

Now the venom in his voice was unmistakable.

As Norina did as he told her, she thought she could understand exactly what he was feeling.

A woman had treated him as treacherously as she had been treated by Violet.

The flames devoured the two letters she had flung into the fire. As they did so, Norina wished she could destroy in the same way the ties which bound her to her stepmother.

"They are . . . both utterly . . . despicable!" she told herself.

chapter four

DESPITE the *Marquis*'s resolution to escape from London, they were not able to leave until the next day.

The Courier who was engaged to arrange the journey explained that it would be impossible, at such short notice, to obtain cabins on the Cross-Channel Steamer.

Nor, he pointed out, for the French to attach the *Marquis*'s private coach to the Express train to Paris.

Grudgingly the *Marquis* conceded that he would wait another day.

He gave strict instructions to Jean that nobody was to know that he was still in residence.

Norina, by this time, had learnt that the house belonged to Lord Winterburn, who was a friend of the *Marquis*'s.

He was abroad and had lent him the house while he wished to remain in London.

The man-servant was also the Caretaker and his wife the Cook.

Surprisingly Norina found the food delicious. She discovered that most of it had been prepared by Jean.

She had expected to eat alone, but when it was time to dress for dinner the *Marquis* said:

"If you dine with me, I can go on discussing any further business there is to be done."

He said it sharply, almost as if he resented the fact that she would be with him.

However, Norina only answered quietly:

"Merci, Monsieur."

She thought with a smile of amusement that the black evening-gown she had bought would come in useful after all, although, of course, the *Marquis* would not be able to see her in it.

It was, in fact, very becoming, more so, she thought, than the white gowns she had worn as a *débutante*.

She wondered a little wistfully if she would ever wear those again.

It was depressing to think of the large amount of money her father had expended on her.

It reminded her again that she must be very careful with what she possessed. It had to last for a long time.

She was already afraid that when they arrived in Paris, the *Marquis* would dispense with her services.

Then she would have to look around for other employment as well as a place to stay.

As if she were talking to her father, she said to herself:

"It is always a mistake to be frightened by a fence before one has to jump it. I shall just have to wait and see what turns up."

It was a relief, at any rate, to know she could eat

74

everything that was served at the table instead of being afraid she was being poisoned.

It was difficult to think of what had happened last night without feeling a sense of panic sweep over her.

Then she told herself that she had to behave calmly and coolly. It was what her mother would have expected.

Lady Sedgewyn had often said to her:

"Royalty always behaves with dignity in public. They do not cry at Funerals or at any other time, and they keep themselves strictly under control, even if they are shot at or bombs are dropped near their carriages."

Norina was aware that Queen Victoria had behaved with great bravery when a young man had shot at her in the Park. She told herself that one could not be certain of anything.

Even the *Marquis,* who, she was sure, was a most unlikely person, had been shot by a jealous husband.

It was impossible to think of a worse punishment than to be blinded for life.

At dinner the *Marquis* talked quickly and dispassionately on a number of subjects. None of them were in the least personal.

Fortunately Norina was used to discussing Political and International Affairs with her father. She did not therefore feel at a loss during the conversation.

In fact, she surprised the *Marquis* with her knowledge of recent events in France.

She thought with a little smile that he was unlikely to suspect her of being as young as she actually was.

Dinner was not a long meal. The *Marquis* had everything cut into small pieces by Jean.

He ate elegantly. She knew he was determined to appear as natural as possible.

When dinner was finished, she retired to bed because she was, in fact, very tired.

When she took off her wig, she brushed her hair, said her prayers, got into bed, and fell asleep almost immediately.

*   *   *

Norina was woken by the woman who was married to the man-servant pulling back the curtains.

"Breakfast 'll be ready in 'alf-an-'our, Ma'am," she said.

She left a can of hot water on the wash-stand and went from the room.

Norina wondered if she had noticed her hair. Then she remembered that the woman had not seen her before and would therefore not be surprised.

She, however, fixed her wig very carefully. It would be disastrous if the *Marquis* was told she was disguising herself in any way.

At breakfast he said very little until they had finished.

Then the Courier who had been given instructions the previous day came into the room.

"I thought I should tell you, *Monsieur le Marquis*," he said very politely, "that I have managed to engage the two best cabins aboard the Cross-Channel Steamer, and have received this morning a telegram from France to say that your private coach will be attached to the afternoon train."

"Thank you," the *Marquis* replied. "You made

76

sure that no one was aware of my identity?''

''I booked the accommodation at Victoria and in the Steamer in the name of *le Comte de Soisson*.''

''Very good,'' the *Marquis* replied.

The man bowed and left the room, and the *Marquis* said as if he were speaking to himself:

''The difficulty now will be for me to board the Steamer without anybody noticing me.''

Norina thought, then she asked:

''Might I make a suggestion?''

''What is it?'' the *Marquis* asked.

''Because you are tall, people are bound to notice your bandage, but, if you were in a wheel-chair, people will merely think you are an old man.''

''That is a very intelligent suggestion,'' the *Marquis* remarked. ''I cannot imagine why I did not think of it myself.''

He sent Norina quickly to find out if the Courier had left the house. Fortunately he was still there.

The *Marquis* explained to him what he needed. The Courier said he would arrange for a wheel-chair both at Dover and Calais.

The *Marquis* then allowed Norina to lead him to the Study, where a large number of letters had arrived by the morning post.

There were invitations, which the *Marquis* ordered to be answered in the same way as those of yesterday, and circulars.

Norina had been given a small room off the hall as an office.

She was about to go there when Jean came into the Study with a note on a silver salver.

''What is it?'' the *Marquis* asked.

"A note, *Monsieur*," Jean replied, "delivered by a groom."

The *Marquis* stiffened.

Jean, without being told, passed the silver salver to Norina.

She saw at once that the note was written in the same hand and on the same writing-paper as the two letters she had burned yesterday.

She waited until Jean had left the room before she said:

"I think, *Monsieur*, this letter comes from the Lady who waited for you last night. Do you wish me to read it?"

To her surprise the *Marquis* asked:

"What do you suggest?"

She looked at him, wondering if he really wanted to know her opinion.

Realising he was waiting, she said after a moment:

"Let me . . . throw it on . . . the fire. It will only . . . hurt you to think of . . . what happened, and the . . . sooner you . . . forget it the better!"

"Do you really think I can forget that I am blind?" the *Marquis* asked.

"You are not *permanently* blind," Norina insisted, "you are only inconvenienced by not being able to see as clearly as you would wish to do."

She spoke impulsively, and the *Marquis* said:

"Why should you be so sure that my sight will not be impaired?"

"It is something I feel so strongly that I know I am correct in saying that within a few weeks you will be able to forget that this ever happened and just be yourself again."

The *Marquis* smiled.

For the first time it was not the bitter, cynical smile that had twisted his lips yesterday.

"You certainly think in an original way, *Madame*," he said, "and you are encouraging me to be optimistic."

"You would be very stupid to be anything else," Norina replied. "If your eyes really were badly damaged with no hope of recovery, the Oculists would have told you so when they first examined them. It is therefore only a question of patience, which is irksome but not soul-destroying!"

The *Marquis* gave a short laugh.

"Thank you, Mrs. Wyndham. You are very wise!"

* * *

It was an hour later that the Oculist called. When Norina knew he was in the house, she prayed that she had not been over-confident.

When she learned that the *Marquis* was alone she went to his Study. She could not wait to know the verdict.

He was sitting in the window in the sunshine, and as she crossed the room, he said:

"Have you come to ask whether you were right or wrong?"

"Of course I have," Norina replied. "You did not send for me, and I could not bear to sit worrying until I knew the truth."

"I am flattered that you should be so interested," the *Marquis* said, "and I am delighted to tell you that you were right. But the Oculist insisted that I continue to wear the bandage."

Norina clasped her hands together.

"That is good news . . . very good . . . news," she cried, "and I am thrilled to know that you will soon be well!"

"Then, of course, I will be able to read my own letters," the *Marquis* said.

Norina was suddenly still.

"Are you . . . saying," she asked in a very small voice, "that it is . . . unnecessary for me to . . . come with you . . . to France?"

"Would it upset you to be left behind?" the *Marquis* enquired.

"Please, take me . . . with you . . . oh . . . please do! I cannot explain . . . but it is very . . . important that I . . . leave London!"

As soon as she spoke she realised she had made a mistake, for the *Marquis* said:

"Tell me why. I thought yesterday that your desire to stay with me was rather strange, but now I find it even stranger that you should wish to leave your own country."

There was silence. Then Norina answered:

"Please . . . do not think me rude . . . but I . . . cannot answer . . . that question."

"You are in trouble," the *Marquis* said. "But I thought your husband was dead."

"He is . . . I am a widow . . . I am wearing mourning . . . for him."

"Then if you are not hiding from your husband— who is it that has frightened you?"

Norina made no reply, and the *Marquis* said:

"I know you are frightened! I can hear it in your voice, and although I am not touching you, I could swear that you are trembling!"

Norina walked a little nearer to the window so that she could look out at the sunshine.

She did not speak, and after some seconds the *Marquis* said:

"I think you owe me an explanation."

"It is . . . something I . . . cannot explain," Norina answered. "Please . . . be understanding and just . . . accept me as a competent Secretary and . . . Reader."

She looked hastily round the Study. The morning newspapers were lying on a stool in front of the fireplace.

"I am sure," she said desperately, "that you would like me to read the newspapers. If I read you the headlines, you can tell me which stories you would like me to read further."

"You are running away," the *Marquis* said, "but you have made me curious and, of course, as I cannot see, I shall have to use my perception, or what you might call my 'Inner Eye' to find out what is worrying you."

"Perhaps that is something which will keep you occupied," Norina said, "and when you do learn the answer, you may find it disappointing."

"I feel that is unlikely," the *Marquis* replied.

Norina picked up the newspapers and started to read some of the headlines.

At the same time, she was no longer trembling. It was obvious that the *Marquis* was taking her with him to France.

The *Marquis* and Norina left early in the morning.

Just in case there was anyone on the platform who might have seen her at a party or a Ball, Norina covered her face with her black veil.

She did the same when they arrived at Dover.

The *Marquis* in his wheel-chair was lifted on board the steamer with Jean pushing and the Courier pulling the chair.

The *Marquis* was wearing an overcoat, the collar of which he pulled up over his chin. His hat came down to cover his face.

Norina followed discreetly behind. She thought that none of the passengers there were in the least curious about an elderly man in a wheel-chair.

All they were concerned with was hurrying aboard and taking the best seats.

She was delighted to find that she had a small, quite comfortable cabin to herself.

The *Marquis* was next door, and there was only one other private cabin on the Steamer.

There was a strong wind, and the sea was choppy even before they left the harbour.

Norina was not certain whether or not she would be a good sailor. She decided not to take any chances.

She therefore took off her hat and lay down on the bunk.

When they left the harbour the sea was very rough. She found her wig which, as she had told Dawes when he brought it to her, was tight. It was so restricting that it gave her a headache.

She therefore took it off to lie down with her eyes closed.

The Steamer pitched and rolled. While at first she was afraid she would be sea-sick, she unexpectedly fell asleep.

*　　*　　*

Norina was awakened by the Courier knocking on the door of the cabin and calling:

"We are in harbour, Mrs. Wyndham, and will be going ashore in a few minutes!"

Norina jumped up hastily.

She had been dreaming that she was on the swing which her father had tied between two trees when she was a little girl.

Quickly she put on her hat and coat. She was just ready when Jean came in to collect her hand-luggage.

"I am taking *Monsieur* ashore first," he said.

Norina thought it a good idea that they should board the train before the other passengers disembarked.

This was obviously the *Marquis*'s idea.

He was pushed at a tremendous pace along the Quay and on to where the train to Paris was waiting.

His private coach was at the very end of the train. Norina, following him, thought there would be no prying eyes to recognise them.

She had never seen a private coach before.

The *Marquis*'s was obviously very comfortable. It had deep armchairs and small tables in front of them on which a meal could be served.

There was a Pantry and, as she was to discover

later, two bedrooms, besides a convenient amount of room for the luggage.

Once they had seated themselves, Jean produced a bottle of champagne.

"I feel this is something we both need," the *Marquis* remarked, "after that very unpleasant crossing."

"I luckily missed it," Norina said, "because I fell asleep!"

"Then you are certainly a better sailor than most women!" the *Marquis* remarked dryly.

Norina had drawn the veil back from her face.

As she lifted the glass of champagne to her lips, she thought she might as well take off her hat. She wanted to be comfortable for the long journey to Paris.

It was then, to her consternation, she realised she had forgotten to replace her wig.

Having taken it off, she had put it down on the berth on which she was lying.

When she got up so hastily she must have thrown the rug which covered her over it, forgetting it was there.

There was nothing she could do.

She hoped that Jean would not mention to the *Marquis* that she had suddenly changed the colour of her hair.

"Perhaps he will not be aware of it," she consoled herself.

At the same time, it was extremely annoying after Dawes had gone to so much trouble in procuring the wig.

It was, however, impossible not to be excited when the train moved out of the station. She was seeing France for the first time.

At first there were the well-cultivated fields which looked very similar to their English counterparts.

Then there was the wide open land.

The broad hedges and the great forests seemed enormous enough to contain the dragons which as a child she had believed lurked in them.

She thought the *Marquis* might be interested to know what they were passing. She therefore detailed to him what she was seeing.

"There is a very unusual Church," she exclaimed "with two spires, and I am sure it must be very old. There is what looks like a Convent or a Monastery on one side of it."

There were picturesque little hamlets that delighted her. Also the long roads with their sentinellike trees on either side.

She described everything she was seeing quite naturally to the *Marquis*. She thought it was a mistake for him to sit brooding over his blindness.

Finally, when darkness fell, Jean brought them their supper from the Pantry. It must have been ordered by the Courier before they started on their journey.

It seemed to Norina to be delightful. But the *Marquis* complained about the soup and was not as enthusiastic as she was over the *pâté*.

"I believe the best cheeses come from Normandy," she said after they had finished a main dish of chicken.

"Who told you that?" the *Marquis* enquired.

"I expect it was my father," Norina replied, "but I have read a great deal about France, and I cannot tell you how exciting it is for me to be here!"

"I am sorry I cannot show you Paris," the *Marquis*

said, "and, of course, you will not be able to wander about by yourself."

"Why not?" Norina asked in surprise.

"Because, Mrs. Wyndham, you are a woman, and I gather, even with your spectacles, a very presentable one!"

"Did Jean . . . tell you . . . that?" Norina asked. "I am . . . flattered!"

"How old are you?" the *Marquis* asked unexpectedly.

Norina drew in her breath.

This was an important question which she knew she would have to answer intelligently.

After a moment she said:

"As a woman you will understand that I do not willingly reveal such personal information about myself, but shall I say we are perhaps, *Monsieur*, somewhat of the same age."

"I shall be thirty next birthday," the *Marquis* said, "which I am sure you will think very old."

"I have always been told," Norina said, "that forty is the youth of old age and the old age of youth!"

The *Marquis* laughed.

"Was it a Frenchman or an Englishman who said that?"

"I am not certain, but I think that a Frenchman would be too polite to probe deeply."

"I stand corrected!" the *Marquis* said. "But as we have nothing else to talk about, tell me a little about .yourself. To begin with, what is your Christian name?"

Norina had already thought of the answer to this.

She had decided it might be dangerous to call herself Norina.

At the same time, she did not wish in an unguarded moment to forget what she had decided her name would be.

She therefore replied "Rina," knowing that was a name that would not slip her mind.

"Rina!" the *Marquis* repeated pensively. "And now tell me about your husband. Did you love him very much?"

"Of course," Norina said quickly, "but I do not want to talk . . . about him . . . or about . . . myself."

"Now you are being difficult again," the *Marquis* said. "I am trying to create a composite picture of you in the darkness of my mind, and I think the least you could do would be to give me some clues. Even in a Paper Chase the runners can look for the paper!"

"That makes it too easy," Norina objected, "and you will just have to find out for yourself!"

She bent forward as she spoke to draw back the curtains over the windows. She looked out into the darkness.

"The stars are coming out," she said, "and the little hamlet we are passing has lights in practically every window. It is very romantic!"

"Is that what you are looking for?" the *Marquis* asked. "Another romance?"

He did not wait for her answer, but went on:

"Of course you are! Love is what every woman wants, and they feel if they do not find it, there is something wrong with them."

"I think the love you are talking about, *Monsieur*,"

Norina said coldly, "is different from the love that I have known in my life."

"Tell me about it," the *Marquis* said.

Norina was thinking of her father and mother as she said:

"Real love, which as you say, is what all women want—is the companionship of the mind, the heart, and the soul."

"And what about the body?" the *Marquis* enquired.

"It is everything, and that, of course, is important, but what really matters is that a man and a woman look for the other half of themselves, and if they find it, then they are blissfully happy for ever."

"It cannot be for ever," the *Marquis* said, "but only until one dies."

Norina shook her head.

"I am quite certain," she said, "that if two people really love each other, then they will be together for eternity. When they are born again, they will not be apart, but will find each other as they did in this life."

"That is the Buddhist theory rather than the Christian," the *Marquis* observed.

"I do not think it matters what it is called," Norina said, "but in Life there cannot be Death."

There was silence for a moment.

Then the *Marquis* said:

"So you are quite certain that is the truth and you will find your husband again?"

Again there was silence.

Norina had not been thinking of herself, but of ideas of love she had read about. It was the way her mother had loved her father.

Yet she was wondering, as she had a million times before, how her father could possibly have married Violet and put her in her mother's place.

It hurt her agonisingly to think of it, so that for a moment she forgot that the *Marquis* was waiting for an answer to his question.

Suddenly he said:

"What is hurting you? Why are you so unhappy? I can feel it as if it were a wave sweeping over me."

Norina was startled.

"You are reading my . . . thoughts!" she said. "And that is something you must . . . not do, and I am . . . sure you would not do . . . if your eyes were not . . . bandaged."

"I thought you approved of me using my 'Inner Eye,'" the *Marquis* said.

"But not where I am concerned!"

"Then for what else?" he enquired. "We are alone together and it would be very boring if we could not talk about fundamental interests rather than stocks and shares!"

Norina laughed.

"I have no wish to talk about them!"

"Surely you are interested in money?" the *Marquis* asked. "And do you realise that you have never asked me what salary I intend to pay you?"

Norina remembered how Dawes had told her that was what she should do.

"It was foolish of me," she admitted, "but it did not . . . seem to matter, apart from the fact that you were . . . taking me . . . away from England."

"I am still waiting to hear what 'Big, Bad Wolf' is frightening you!" the *Marquis* remarked.

Norina thought that Violet was hardly a "Big, Bad Wolf." She was more like a poisonous snake slithering along the ground and making it difficult for her victim to escape.

"But you have escaped!" the *Marquis* said.

Norina gave a little cry.

"Now you are reading my thoughts again, and it is not fair! I shall have shut my eyes and see if I can read yours!"

"I am delighted for you to do so," the *Marquis* said, "and shall I tell you that I am finding this journey far more interesting and definitely more amusing than I expected?"

"Thank you," Norina said, "and it is only fair that you should enjoy it when I am thrilled with every mile as we draw nearer and nearer to Paris."

The *Marquis* did not speak for a little while.

Then he said:

"I am wondering if I am making a mistake."

"About what?" Norina enquired.

"In going to Paris," he said, "I wanted to escape from London because I could not bear to have anybody know what happened to me. But the same applies to Paris. It would be a good story to know that 'The Wicked *Marquis*' has got his 'just deserts' at last!"

" 'The Wicked *Marquis*'?" Norina repeated. "Is that your reputation?"

"It is," the *Marquis* admitted. "I am well aware of what people say about me, and as I find beautiful women irresistible, there are always jealous husbands and other men who quite naturally feel they must defend their honour."

He put up his hands to his bandaged eyes as he

spoke, and the bitterness was back in his voice.

"What you have to do in the future," Norina said, "is to ask yourself if it is worth the risk."

"I am already asking myself that."

"I think the answer is that you should settle down and have a large family," Norina said. "That should keep you occupied when you are in the country."

She paused before she added:

"I expect you have a magnificent *Château* somewhere in France?"

"I have one in the Loire Valley," the *Marquis* replied, "but I have no intention of going there."

"Why not?"

"Because I have a great number of relatives who would exclaim over my wounds and wag their heads and say they always knew something like this would happen sooner or later!"

Because the way he spoke sounded so funny, Norina laughed.

Then she said quickly:

"Forgive me . . . I am not laughing at you . . . but you must admit it is going to be difficult to keep yourself hidden and for anyone not to know what has occurred."

"It cannot be impossible," the *Marquis* said, "and of course you must help me."

She looked at him enquiringly and, realising he was waiting for her reply, she said:

"I will help you in any way I can."

"That is what I wanted to hear," the *Marquis* said, "and of course you understand that my friends and my enemies will accept it as being quite natural if I disappear from Social life provided they believe I have somebody with me who must not be seen."

Norina stared at him.

"Do you . . . mean . . . ?" she began.

"Exactly what you are thinking," the *Marquis* said. "Now, tell me what you look like."

chapter five

NORINA could not think how to answer.

She stared ahead, looking at the wall of the coach as the wheels rumbled on to Paris.

The *Marquis* waited. Then he said:

"Turn your face towards me, Rina."

Because Norina was so bemused, she obeyed him and realised he was sitting sideways to face her.

She had taken off her spectacles because they blurred her vision. She wanted to see the stars and the land through which they were passing.

She would have put them on again, but the *Marquis* reached out and cupped her face with his hands.

A little shiver went through her at his touch, and he said quietly:

"I will not hurt you. I am only trying to find out whether Jean was right in saying you are *très jolie*."

It was impossible for Norina to move.

Still with one hand on her left cheek, the *Marquis* slowly outlined her face with a finger of his right hand.

First he moved it gently over her forehead. She was glad she was not wearing a wig.

Then he outlined her eye-brows and, very slowly so that she was not nervous, slid his finger down to touch the lids of her eyes.

Because she was shy, she shut them. His finger-tip lingered for a second on the length of her eye-lashes.

Then his finger moved down her straight little nose. It paused beneath it before he touched the curves of her lips. First left—right, then her underlip.

She did not understand, but it gave her a strange sensation she had never felt before.

She made a little murmur in her throat. Yet she did not move as he outlined the contour of her chin, rising up finally to her ear.

He touched it. Again she felt something strange streak through her breast. She thought it must be because she was nervous of what he was doing.

Then, so quickly that she was surprised, he released her.

Sitting back again in his seat, he said:

"Jean is right, and I am prepared to wager a large sum that you are, in fact, very lovely."

Because Norina felt strangely shaken by what he had just done, she turned her head away.

She looked out of the window from which the curtains were drawn back.

Her hands still lay in her lap holding her spectacles.

Again unexpectedly the *Marquis* put out his left hand and covered them.

She thought he was going to refer to the fact that she wore spectacles.

Instead, his fingers crept a little lower. Then he said

in the tone of someone who has made a discovery:

"No wedding-ring. It is what I suspected!"

Too late Norina remembered, when Dawes had suggested she should be a widow, that she should have taken her mother's wedding-ring from her jewel-box.

Now that she thought about it, having packed everything she possessed, he would not have forgotten her mother's jewellery. It had been in the safe where her own was kept in a special drawer in her bedroom.

Because she felt she must make some explanation, she said a little lamely:

"I . . . I left it for . . . safety with my other . . . jewellery and forgot to . . . put it on when we . . . left this morning."

"That sounds very plausible," the *Marquis* said, taking his hand away. "But I am suspicious of that mythical husband about whom you say you do not wish to talk."

"I . . . cannot think . . . why," Norina replied.

She meant to speak defiantly. Instead, her voice was soft, very young, and frightened.

"Would it not be best," the *Marquis* asked, "if we had no secrets from each other? After all, you have learned mine."

He spoke in the beguiling voice which most women found irresistible.

Norina had a sudden vision of her stepmother stalking her, waiting to pounce and murder her wherever she might be.

She was sure it would be a mistake to speak of it to anybody, even the *Marquis*.

"I . . . think," she said hesitatingly, "that . . . it

would be safer for . . . me . . . and for you . . . if
we . . . left things . . . as they are.''

"You are determined to make me curious,'' the
Marquis said.

"When we reach . . . Paris I am sure . . . there will
be a . . . great number of . . . other things for . . . you
to think . . . about.''

"Not if I am to isolate myself alone with you. I
shall feel it rather tiresome to be eternally with a
Sphinx who is more enigmatic than any Sphinx has
ever been before!''

"Once you know . . . my secrets,'' Norina argued,
"you will find them very . . . dull and then there will
be . . . nothing to . . . think about, but . . . yourself.''

The *Marquis* laughed.

"You always say the unexpected,'' he said, "and
while I find it infuriating, I am still intrigued. Now,
tell me, beautiful little Rina, what you are going to
do about us.''

Norina glanced at him and glanced away.

She had a feeling that in some subtle manner he
was flirting with her.

It was what she had been told Frenchmen did with
any woman with whom they came in contact.

There was a smile on his lips, and she thought that
when his eyes were not bandaged, he would, in fact,
be exceedingly handsome.

She felt a sudden panic in case she should become
too closely involved with him.

Supposing, as apparently a great number of other
women had, she fell in love with him? Then she would

write him a desperate despairing letter when he no longer had any use for her.

"I must be sensible about this," she told herself, "and I must remember his reputation. To him I am just a Secretary who can never be of any importance in his life."

Because she was so vividly conscious of him sitting next to her, she rose a little unsteadily to her feet.

"I think I would . . . like to go and . . . lie down," she said. "We have a long way to go, and the movement of the train is making me sleepy."

"I am sure that is sensible," the *Marquis* agreed. "It will be nearly midnight when we arrive in Paris. We could stay in a siding until the morning, but I would rather move out of the train when it is dark so that we will not be noticed."

"I am . . . sure that is a . . . good idea," Norina agreed.

She walked across the coach and found her way into one of the small bedrooms attached to it.

She had left her widow's hat on the bed. Now she put it on a chair and stretched herself out.

She intended to go to sleep.

Instead she kept feeling the *Marquis*'s fingers moving over her skin.

She could still feel the strange sensation he had evoked in her breast when he touched her lips.

"Please . . . God . . . do not let . . . me fall . . . in love with . . . him," she prayed, "but let me . . . stay working for . . . him. I like being with him. I like talking to him . . . but whatever . . . happens, I

97

must . . . not think of . . . him as a . . . man, but . . .
just as . . . my employer.''

       *   *   *

It was, as the *Marquis* had warned Norina, very late
when they arrived in Paris.

He insisted that they wait in the coach until practically all the passengers had left the train.

Then they walked slowly down the platform to
where, outside the *Gare du Nord,* a carriage was waiting.

Norina only had time to notice before they stepped
into it that the horses were very well bred. The uniforms of the servants were exceedingly smart.

Jean jumped up on the box beside the footman. The
Courier stayed behind to see to the luggage.

Although it was late, there were still lights in a
great many windows.

People were moving about in the street, and every
so often there was the sound of music.

There was also a considerable amount of traffic.

To Norina it was all very exciting.

She sat forward, looking out of the window, thinking that Paris was all she had expected it to be. There
was some irresistible magic in the air.

They passed the Opera House, and she recognised
it from the pictures she had seen.

Then they went down what she was sure was the
Rue de la Paix before they reached the *Place Ven-
dôme*.

Two minutes later she gave a little cry of excitement
because they were in the *Place de la Concorde*.

The fountains were playing and the lights made the water thrown up into the air iridescent and luminous.

"It is lovely . . . perfectly lovely!" she exclaimed. "Oh, thank you, thank you for bringing me here!"

"I thought that was what you would feel," the *Marquis* said in a deep voice.

"How could anyone not be thrilled by the *Place de la Concorde*?" Norina asked.

The *Marquis* did not answer.

The light from one of the street lamps illuminated his face, and she saw he was smiling.

They only had a short distance to go before the horses turned off the *Champs-Élysées*. A moment later they passed through some iron gates and up a short drive.

"Is this where you live?" Norina asked. "I have read that the houses in the *Champs-Élysées* are the most distinguished in the whole of Paris."

"That is what I like to think," the *Marquis* replied.

The horses came to a standstill and a number of servants appeared.

There were footmen in white wigs and very elaborate uniforms.

Norina got out first.

Then Jean assisted the *Marquis* to alight, and led him by the arm into the house.

A *Majordomo* more resplendent than the other servants greeted him respectfully. Norina was aware that he was looking at his Master's bandaged eyes in consternation.

"We are tired," the *Marquis* said, "and will go straight upstairs to bed."

"There is food and wine in the *Salon, Monsieur le Marquis,*" the *Majordomo* replied.

"I want nothing," the *Marquis* said firmly, "but perhaps *Madame* Wyndham would like . . . ?"

"No, no," Norina interrupted. "Thank you very much, but I, too, would like to go to bed."

The Housekeeper was waiting at the top of the stairs to show her to a bedroom. It was on the First Floor and exceedingly luxurious.

Norina wondered if the Courier had been told she was to be treated more as a guest than a Secretary.

A maid unpacked her nightgown and what she needed, and helped her out of her clothes.

As soon as she was in the big bed, which was very comfortable, Norina fell asleep.

But her last thought was that she must not become too involved with the *Marquis*.

*　　*　　*

When Norina awoke, it was morning. Her breakfast was brought in and set beside her bed.

It was, she thought, a delight and exactly what she expected.

There were deliciously light hot *croissants* with a variety of different *confitures* or honey to spread on them.

The coffee tasted better than any she had ever tasted before.

When she sat back against her pillows she could see the sunshine shimmering on the trees outside. The sky above them was very blue.

Because it was so exciting, she jumped out of bed and ran to the window.

"Whatever the *Marquis* might say," she told herself, "I have to explore Paris, and if there is no one to go with me, I shall go alone!"

She then remembered she had duties to perform. She rang for a maid, who brought her hot water and helped her dress.

She went downstairs, wondering if her relationship with the *Marquis* would be in any way different from how it had been before.

He was waiting for her in a magnificent *Salon*.

It was decorated with what she was sure was Louis XIV furniture and pictures which she longed to inspect.

She was, however, determined to be businesslike, and when she entered the room she said:

"*Bonjour, Monsieur!* I am sure in your absence there must be a large amount of correspondence awaiting your attention, and I am wondering where I might find it."

"I have already thought of that," the *Marquis* replied, "and my permanent Secretary has dealt with all but those of an obviously personal nature."

Norina started.

"Y-your permanent . . . Secretary?" she repeated. "Then . . . you do not . . . need me?"

She felt, as she spoke, as if the ceiling had suddenly crashed down on her head. The sunshine had vanished.

"My permanent Secretary," the *Marquis* explained, "also runs my house, but he does not deal with my private correspondence."

"Then you do . . . still need . . . me?"

"I will tell you when you are no longer necessary," the *Marquis* replied.

The relief made Norina for a moment feel weak. Without waiting to be told she could do so, she sat down on a chair.

"You . . . frightened . . . me!" she said accusingly.

"You frightened yourself," the *Marquis* replied. "You might not have noticed, but my eyes are still bandaged!"

"I can . . . hardly say that I am . . . glad," Norina said in a voice that shook.

"Then suppose you do your duty," the *Marquis* suggested, "and open the letters that are standing on that *Secrétaire* by the window?"

Norina rose and walked to where she could now see a large pile of letters.

It was obvious that they were private and personal. She thought some of the envelopes were scented as . . . Patsy's . . . had been.

She picked them up with a letter-opener that lay beside them and turned round.

The *Marquis* was now sitting in a high-backed armchair. With his legs crossed and very elegantly dressed he looked like a *Grand Seigneur*.

She walked nearer to him. Sitting down in a chair, she slit open the first envelope.

As she did so, the *Marquis* asked:

"What are you wearing?"

"My black gown."

"I think that is a mistake."

She looked at him in surprise.

"Why?"

"I have already told you that you are my excuse for not receiving my friends, and therefore you must look the part."

Norina stared and he went on:

"Servants talk, and nothing can prevent them from doing so. By to-night a great number of people in Paris will know that I have returned home. They will also learn that I wish to receive no visitors. The question they will inevitably ask themselves is why? Do you understand?"

"Y-yes . . . yes . . . of course," Norina said hesitatingly.

"Then I suggest," the *Marquis* said, "that either you put on a gown that is not black, or if you do not have one with you, then I will provide it."

"No . . . no . . . of course . . . not!" Norina protested. "I could not allow you to . . . pay for . . . my clothes. It would be most . . . improper! As it happens . . . I have some very . . . pretty gowns . . . with me."

"And who paid for those?" the *Marquis* enquired.

"My father," Norina said automatically.

Because suddenly she guessed what he suspected, she said:

"I do not . . . want to take . . . part in this . . . Masquerade. It is very . . . embarrassing."

"You would prefer to find someone else?" the *Marquis* asked coldly.

Norina drew in her breath.

She knew he was saying that if she did not do what he wanted, she could leave.

But how could she do that with nowhere to go?

Quickly, because she was frightened, she said:

"I will . . . do what . . . you want, but I am . . . afraid of making a mistake which would . . . hurt you."

"I think really," the *Marquis* answered, "you are worrying about your own reputation."

"No, that is . . . not true," Norina said. "My reputation is of . . . no importance, and I can say . . . that in all honesty."

She was thinking as she spoke that it was true, because what she was doing was saving her life.

If she were gossiped about or unkind things were said, it would hardly be of any consequence if she was dead.

As if he were reading her thoughts again, the *Marquis* said:

"Now, suppose we go back to the beginning and let me ask you, because you promised to help me, to make yourself look as pretty and attractive as possible."

He paused, then went on:

"As you are married, your husband has gone Big Game Hunting or is visiting America and is not aware you are here with me in Paris."

Norina stared at him, then she laughed.

"Why are you laughing?" the *Marquis* asked.

"Because everything is becoming . . . more and more complicated," Norina replied, "and I am going to find it difficult remembering which is . . . really me, or just . . . part of a . . . Fairy Tale."

"In which case, I am obviously the 'Bold, Bad Villain'!" the *Marquis* said.

"I have not . . . said so, and I think . . . if you are honest . . . you are . . . fishing for . . . compliments!"

"I can hardly be 'Prince Charming,' " the *Marquis* answered, "with my eyes bandaged, unable to see how beautiful the Princess is, who is also in hiding."

"It is . . . your story," Norina answered, "so, of course, you can . . . play any part in it . . . you choose. I am quite willing to be 'Cinderella' after the Fairy Godmother waved her . . . magic wand and changed . . . her rags into a . . . beautiful gown."

"You shall go and change it as soon as you have opened my letters," the *Marquis* said. "There will be no one to see you in the house, but descriptions of you will be carried on the wind, as they inevitably are."

It all sounded so ridiculous that Norina laughed again.

"I am sure I am . . . dreaming!" she said. "This . . . cannot be . . . true!"

"Then let us hope you do not wake up to anything unpleasant," the *Marquis* said somewhat mockingly.

"I do not . . . believe there is anything . . . unpleasant in . . . Paris!"

She opened the *Marquis*'s letters and read them aloud.

Quite a number of them were from Ladies begging him to let them know as soon as he returned. They all told him how miserable they had been in his absence.

There was a repetition about them.

It made Norina think that intelligent and witty as Frenchwomen were reputed to be, there was a lamentable sameness in the way they expressed themselves when they were in love.

The *Marquis* made no comment as she went from one letter to another.

Finally, when she had read the last one, he said:

"Put them on the fire!"

"You . . . you do not . . . wish me to . . . answer any of . . . them?"

"There is nothing to say."

She rose to her feet and put the letters one by one into the fire. The flames flared up and the pages of passion curled beneath them.

When the last one had burned to ashes she turned away.

"What are you thinking?" the *Marquis* asked.

"I am . . . feeling sorry for . . . those women," Norina answered.

"And for me?"

"There is no reason why I should feel sorry for you, but they are tributes at your feet, or incense, if you prefer, from worshippers before your shrine."

She spoke lightly, and only as she finished speaking did she think she had been rude.

"I am . . . sorry," she said quickly, "that is . . . something I should . . . not have . . . said."

"Always the unexpected!" the *Marquis* remarked. "Go and change."

Norina ran upstairs.

She found that without instructions, the maid had unpacked several of her trunks.

The gowns which her father had bought for her in London were hanging in the wardrobe.

She felt it embarrassing to have to explain why she was changing so soon. She therefore managed to undo her gown herself.

She put on a pretty summer gown which she also managed to button up at the back.

She thought it was suitable for a young girl and not for the married woman she was supposed to be.

As she expected, Dawes had packed her jewellery as well as her mother's.

The cases were standing on a beautifully inlaid commode.

She looked into her mother's box and found, as she should have done before, her wedding-ring.

She put it on her finger. Because it was a little large, she made sure it would stay on by adding one of her mother's smaller diamond rings.

Also, to make herself look older, she put on a pair of pearl and diamond ear-rings. They had also belonged to her mother.

Shutting the jewel-box, she went back downstairs.

The *Marquis* was still in the room where she had left him, but standing at the open window.

She felt that he was longing to be outside, perhaps driving in the *Bois* or riding one of his horses.

When he heard her approach, he turned round slowly, and as she went towards him, he asked:

"You have changed?"

"I am wearing white with a skirt that is decorated with broderie anglais, and there is a blue sash round my waist."

The *Marquis* did not speak, and she added:

"I am also wearing the wedding-ring which I told you was in my jewel-box."

She spoke defiantly because she still had no wish for him to know how young she was. She was not, whatever he said, prepared to admit that she was not married.

The *Marquis* took her hand in both of his and felt her rings.

"Diamonds?" he questioned. "If your husband was a rich man, why are you forced to work for your living?"

There was no answer to this, and Norina did not reply.

He put up his hand again as if towards her cheek, but instead he touched her ear.

"Ear-rings!" he exclaimed. "And of course you could have sold them rather than become a Secretary."

"Now you are questioning the old 'me,'" Norina said reluctantly. "I thought we had moved into another world in which I am a rich, important social figure who has eloped with you to the Continent."

"Yes, of course," the *Marquis* agreed. "Forgive me. We must, of course, act out our parts and be careful not to forget them."

He put his arm around Norina as he spoke. Before she could realise what was happening, he pulled her against him.

She looked up at him in amazement, then realised he was about to kiss her.

His lips had almost touched hers when she cried:

"Non! Non!"

She fought herself free and moved away from the *Marquis* to the other side of the window. She held on to the window-sill to support herself.

He was standing where she had left him. She

thought, although she was not certain, he was astonished by her reaction to his advances.

She was breathing quickly and was not certain what she should do.

Then the *Marquis* said quietly:

"I thought you had agreed to play the part I have assigned to you."

"But . . . we were only . . . pretending!" Norina managed to gasp.

"Then of course I must apologise," the *Marquis* said, "and may I suggest in my own defence, Rina, that if any other woman had been in your position, she would have thought it very remiss if I had not kissed her in gratitude for her help."

"But . . . you must not . . . kiss me!"

"Why not?"

"Because . . . it would be . . . wrong."

"Why wrong?"

It was a question that was difficult to answer, and Norina said:

"I think one . . . should . . . kiss only somebody with whom . . . they are very much . . . in love."

The *Marquis* smiled.

"Surely it would not be difficult for us to pretend to be in love, at least while we are acting a Play in which it is actually a necessity?"

"I . . . I do not think . . . that is . . . true!" Norina said. "And . . . please . . . I do not . . . want you to . . . kiss me."

She thought if the *Marquis* kissed her, it would give her the same feelings as when he had touched her lips with his fingers.

Then she might easily fall in love with him.

That would mean nothing but misery in the future.

She might find herself writing the sort of letters which "Patsy" and the other women wrote when he was no longer interested in them.

"That is a plea which, of course, I cannot refuse," the *Marquis* said quietly.

He put out a hand to find the back of a chair. He guided himself back to where he had been sitting before.

Then he paused.

"Do not be so frightened, Rina," he said. "I will not hurt you. I assure you, I have never forced myself on any woman who is unwilling."

"H-how do you . . . know I am . . . frightened?" Norina asked in a childlike little voice.

"I can feel it," the *Marquis* answered.

As he spoke, he moved not in the direction of his chair, but towards her.

He stood in front of her before he said:

"Give me your hand."

She held out her hand and his fingers closed over hers.

"I have no wish to cause you any distress," he said gently. "Just trust me and we can, I am sure, be happy together."

As he finished speaking, he raised her hand to his lips.

It was the perfunctory gesture for a Frenchman, but for a second she felt his mouth against her skin.

Instantly there was that same strange sensation within her breast she had felt before.

It made her quiver.

As if the *Marquis* were aware of it, he released her

hand and turned awkwardly in the direction of the fireplace.

She knew he was groping to find something to support him. Automatically she moved forward to take his arm and guide him to his chair.

As he seated himself he said:

"Thank you, Rina, I am very grateful to you."

"That is . . . really what I . . . should be . . . saying to . . . you," Norina replied.

The *Marquis* smiled.

"Then at least we have one thing in common!"

* * *

Luncheon was delicious and served in the most attractive small Dining-Room Norina had ever imagined.

As they moved back to the *Salon* with Jean assisting the *Marquis,* he said:

"We can hardly stay cooped up in the house all day. Where shall we go, Jean?"

Jean shook his head.

"There is nowhere, *Monsieur,* where you would not be seen."

"I need some air."

"If *Monsieur* sat in the garden behind the bushes, he would be invisible except perhaps for two windows on that side of the house."

"Then that is where I shall go," the *Marquis* said. "Are you coming too, Rina?"

"I would like to join you," Norina said, "but may I first write a letter which I want posted at once?"

"Of course!" the *Marquis* agreed.

She went to the *Secrétaire* and wrote a short note
to Dawes. She told him where she was staying and
with whom, adding:

*Thank you so very much for all you have done
for me. It is very exciting being in Paris and
please, let me know if there is any news.*

She signed it just with her initials and addressed
the envelope to Mr. Dawes, c/o Mrs. Rolo.

The *Marquis* had gone out into the garden, but Jean
had come back to wait for her letter.

"Will you please post it immediately," she asked,
"and send it to London by the quickest route possible?"

"I'll see to it, *Madame*."

He took the letter from her and added:

"It's good for *Monsieur* to have someone to talk
to."

"I am afraid he will find it very restricting after a
little while," Norina said.

"*Monsieur*'s eyes grow better every day," Jean
replied, "but he must do as he is told and keep them
bandaged."

He spoke as if he almost suspected Norina of trying
to encourage the *Marquis* to remove the bandage.

Then she guessed that Jean was used to women who
wanted his Master to admire them, and they would
resent the fact that he could not see them.

"*Monsieur* must certainly try to obey the Oculist's
orders," she said aloud, and Jean smiled at her.

He walked away. She was just tidying away the

112

writing-paper and putting the pen back on the tray when the door opened.

She thought Jean must have returned to say there was something wrong with her letter.

But when she looked round it was not Jean who had come into the room.

Instead, there was a smartly dressed man who she knew was French even before he spoke.

He looked around the *Salon* before he asked:

"I thought Alexus would be here. Who, may I ask, *Madame*, are you?"

Norina rose from the chair.

"The *Marquis* is not receiving people at the moment, *Monsieur*."

The Frenchman laughed.

"He will receive me. I am one of his oldest friends. I thought he must be up to some mischief when I heard he was in Paris and had not notified me of his return."

"He has notified no one, *Monsieur*," Norina replied, "because, as I have already said, he is entertaining no one and wishes to be alone."

The Frenchman smiled again.

"Except, *Madame*, for you! You, of course, are the exception."

"*Oui, Monsieur*, that is correct," Norina said, "and so, may I ask you to leave. I will, however, inform *Monsieur le Marquis* that you have called, if you would be so kind as to give me your name."

The Frenchman was obviously astounded at what she said and just stared at her before he said:

"I am *le Vicomte Leporte*, and as I have already

told you, *Madame,* Alexus's oldest friend. I have no intention of being turned away as if I were an intruder!''

"But that, *Monsieur,* is exactly what you are!'' Norina retorted. "So I can only beg you to accept my assurance that the *Marquis* has no wish to see anyone for the moment."

She spoke very politely, at the same time firmly.

The *Vicomte* stood looking indecisive.

She knew he was wondering whether he should defy her or not, and she held out her hand.

"*Au revoir, Monsieur le Vicomte!*" she said. "I hope we shall meet again in more congenial circumstances."

Slowly and with obvious reluctance the *Vicomte* took her hand and bowed over it.

Then he walked to the door. As he reached it, he said:

"Tell Alexus I do not forgive him for this, but having seen you, *Madame,* I understand the reason for his seclusion."

He walked out of the room as he spoke, and Norina heard him going down the passage.

She waited until she was certain he must have left the house.

Then quickly she ran out into the garden to where she knew the *Marquis* was sitting behind some bushes.

The sunshine was warm on her face as she sped out and across the lawn.

It was not difficult to guess where the *Marquis* would be sitting.

She turned to where in the distance she could see

a yew hedge behind which she was certain he had isolated himself.

She ran, and when she reached him, she found he was sitting on a wooden seat on which there were satin cushions.

He was holding his head up into the sunshine which was percolating through the trees.

She was almost breathless as she sat down beside him, saying:

"There is . . . trouble, and . . . I have come to . . . tell you what . . . I have . . . done!"

"Trouble?" the *Marquis* questioned. "What has happened?"

Her breath was still coming in gasps as Norina related exactly what had occurred since he had left the *Salon*.

When she mentioned the *Vicomte*'s name, the *Marquis* gave an exclamation.

"Ramon Leporte! A very old friend, but one of the biggest gossips in the whole of Paris! How the devil did he find out I was here?"

"You said . . . the word would be . . . 'carried on the wind'!" Norina replied.

"I knew I had made a mistake in coming to Paris," he said. "The servants are so damned silly, and whatever I say they will allow my friends, if they are important enough, to enter the house."

"Then . . . what will you do?" Norina asked.

"We will leave!" the *Marquis* said. "And the sooner the better!"

"L-leave? But we have only just arrived. Where can we go?"

"Where I should have gone in the first place," the *Marquis* answered, "to my new Villa in the South of France!"

Norina's eyes widened.

"Can we really go there?"

"That is what we are doing," the *Marquis* said firmly, "so go back to the house and tell the *Major-domo* to send for a Courier—not the one we have just used—but a man who is called Breste."

The *Marquis* gave the order sharply, and Norina rose from the seat.

"I will do as you say," she said, "although I am sad that I shall not see Paris."

"If you are very good," the *Marquis* said, "and do not make a fuss, I will tell you what we will do. When it is dark, we will drive along the Seine, see Nôtre-Dame and come back along the Rue de l'Opéra, when everything will be lit up and be far more glamorous than it looks in the daytime."

Norina clasped her hands together.

"Can we do that?"

"I never break my promises," the *Marquis* said, "and I hope one day I will be able to show you Paris properly when I can see it myself."

"That will be . . . wonderful!" Norina exclaimed.

At the same time, she thought it would be something that was very unlikely to happen.

When the *Marquis* could see again, she would have to leave him.

She felt a sudden depression at the thought.

Then she told herself it was no use looking ahead.

She would have a glimpse of Paris, then she would

go on to see what she had always longed to see—the South of France.

"I am lucky . . . very . . . very . . . lucky!" she was saying as she ran back towards the house to carry out the *Marquis*'s orders.

chapter six

DAWES came out of his Master's room and paused at the top of the stairs. He saw Bolton letting two men into the house.

He thought they looked strange, especially one of them. He watched them as they moved across the hall and were shown into the Drawing-Room.

Bolton came up the stairs to inform Lady Sedgewyn, who had not yet left her bedroom, that she had visitors.

As he reached the top of the stairs, Dawes said to him:

"Who are those two men calling in the morning?"

"One of them's a queer-looking Monk," Bolton answered, "and the other looks to me like a ferret."

He walked past Dawes to knock on Her Ladyship's door.

The word "ferret" made Dawes think, as he had last week, Lady Sedgewyn was employing a Detective to search for Norina.

She and Lord Sedgewyn had at first not been particularly perturbed that Norina was staying with friends.

But when they heard nothing from her, Lord Sedgewyn began to grow anxious about her disappearance.

"Where the devil is my daughter?" he asked Dawes. "It is not like her to upset me or to leave London when she has a number of engagements. The Countess tells me she has been expecting every evening to take her to some Ball or other."

Dawes was wise and said nothing.

He thought, however, that Lady Sedgewyn seemed even more perturbed than her husband. He guessed the reason for it.

Now he slipped along the passage and entered an Ante-Room next to the Drawing-Room. It was rarely used, except as a card-room when there was a large party.

He shut the door by which he had entered and tiptoed across the room.

Very gently he eased open the communicating door of the Drawing-Room.

As soon as he had done so, he could hear the two men talking.

He heard the one he thought looked like a ferret say:

"Now, this is just up your street, and I expects you to remember me when you gets the girl in your hands."

"You'll not be forgotten," the Monklike man replied.

He spoke English but with a definite foreign accent.

They then whispered together in such low voices that Dawes could not hear what they said.

A few minutes later the door opened and Lady Sedgewyn came in.

"Good-morning, Mr. Wentover," she said. "I have been wondering when you would call on me."

"I was waiting," the man called Wentover replied, "until I had some news for Your Ladyship, an' now you'll be very pleased."

"That is what I am hoping!" Lady Sedgewyn replied.

She must have glanced at the other man present because Wentover said:

"May I introduce Father Jacques of the Convent of St. Francis."

"It's a pleasure to meet Your Ladyship," the Monk said slowly.

"Will you sit down," Lady Sedgewyn suggested, "and then, Mr. Wentover, you can tell me what I am waiting to hear."

Dawes put an ear to the crack in the door as the Detective began:

"Following Your Ladyship's instructions, we made every possible enquiry as to the whereabouts of Miss Sedgewyn. We found that she bought a widow's hat at an Emporium in Oxford Street, and wore it the next morning to travel with the *Marquis de Carlamont* to Paris."

"With the *Marquis*?" Lady Sedgewyn exclaimed.

"That's right, Ma'am. He has, as we understand it, suffered an accident to his eyes. They was bandaged and he travelled incognito on the Steamer."

"And my stepdaughter, Norina, was with him? But why?"

"That we have not yet ascertained," Mr. Wentover replied, "except that as he's blind he might have needed somebody to guide him."

"I do not understand," Lady Sedgewyn murmured.

"They arrived in Paris, but after two days," Mr. Wentover continued, "they left for the South of France, where the *Marquis* has a Villa he's recently built on a small promontory called Cap d'Estelle."

"You are quite sure that my stepdaughter is with him?" Lady Sedgewyn asked.

"There's no possibility of my being mistaken," Mr. Wentover answered, "but this, My Lady, is where Father Jacques can be of great help."

Lady Sedgewyn looked at the Monk.

He was rather dissolute-looking, she thought, with bags under his eyes. It made her suspect he was a heavy drinker.

At the same time, she was obviously eager to know what part he was to play.

"It's very fortunate," Mr. Wentover was saying, "that Father Jacques happened to be in England, on a mission which he'll not mind telling you concerns the death of the Earl of Kingswood's daughter."

"The young lady entered my Convent as a postulant," Father Jacques explained, "but she unfortunately succumbed to a fever, which often occurs in the South of France, and died."

Lady Sedgewyn was thinking quickly.

She remembered hearing that the Earl was an avid gambler and ran up enormous debts at the green baize tables.

She also recalled that his daughter had been an heiress.

"You say the Earl's daughter died while in your Convent," she said to the Monk. "What happened to her money?"

There was a little pause before Father Jacques replied:

"It is usual for the Postulants to make over all their worldly goods to the Convent, but in that instance, because of a previous arrangement, half of what the Lady Imogen owned will go to her father."

There was a pregnant pause.

Then Lady Sedgewyn said:

"If my stepdaughter is taken to your Convent, I am prepared to give you two thousand pounds now for your expenses in finding her, and ten thousand pounds on her death as well as another ten thousand pounds when my husband leaves this life."

Father Jacques nodded his head.

"I understand, My Lady, and I will immediately, on my return to France—and I leave to-morrow morning—get in touch with Your Ladyship's stepdaughter."

There was a short pause before he added:

"I am sure she can be—*persuaded* to worship in our Convent, which is very near to the Cap d'Estelle."

He accentuated the word "persuaded".

Dawes did not wait to hear any more.

He slipped out of the Ante-Room and left the house by the back door.

He hurried all the way to the Post Office which was in Mount Street.

When he reached it, he said to the man behind the counter:

"I want to send a telegram to France."

"To France?" the man repeated rather stupidly.

"Yes, France, and don't let there be any mistake about it!" Dawes said.

He was handed the proper form and very laboriously, because he was not a fluent writer, completed it.

He was surprised at the charge, but fortunately he had enough money with him.

Then, wiping his forehead, he left the Post Office and walked slowly back to the house.

* * *

Norina finished dinner and said to the *Marquis*:

"That was the most delicious meal I have ever tasted, but then, I say that every night."

"The new Chef is certainly worth his wages," the *Marquis* replied, "and we must thank Jean for finding him."

Norina looked round the small Dining-Room. The windows opened onto a wide balcony which overlooked the garden.

She had never imagined that anything could be so lovely as the Villa the *Marquis* had just finished building.

Cap d'Estelle was a small promontory between Eze and Cap Ferrat on which there was just room for a Villa and a small garden.

It was usual for Noblemen who built their Villas in

the South of France to set them high up above the sea between Nice and Monte Carlo.

But the *Marquis* five years earlier had seen the promontory. He realised it was for sale and started building.

The Villa, Norina thought when she first saw it, owed something to the Greek Temples, also to an imagination which incorporated the natural landscape.

To reach the Villa one descended from the main road down a twisting drive.

Then the house itself started half-way towards the rock which protruded out into the sea, and on this the *Marquis* was now forming a garden.

When they reached the Villa there was what appeared to be the Ground Floor, yet there was another below it, and two floors above.

It was far too large for a man alone. But as the *Marquis* pointed out, he had innumerable relatives who would, when it was completed, continually wish to borrow it from him.

"It is so lovely and so quiet that I feel people chattering and, of course, gossiping would spoil it," Norina said.

"I am certainly thankful that we have it to ourselves at the moment," the *Marquis* remarked, "and, in fact, at this time of the year there are few people to gossip or chatter because this part of France is fashionable only in the Spring."

"Well, I would rather·be here now!" Norina said.

"It certainly suits our purpose," the *Marquis* agreed.

He rose from the table and walked out onto the balcony which surrounded the Villa.

There was a long flight of marble steps that led from the centre of it down into the garden. There, surprisingly, there were large trees and flower-beds which had just been planted between the rocks.

What entranced Norina when she arrived was that there were climbing geraniums everywhere, also a great number of clematis of every sort, flowering over the rocks and even encircling some of the trees.

"It is a Fairyland!" she declared.

The *Marquis* smiled at the rapture in her voice.

Now the sun had just set and the sky was still crimson. The first evening stars were twinkling directly overhead.

"Tell me what you are seeing," the *Marquis* said quietly.

"I am looking to where the crimson fingers of the sun touch the sea. That is the horizon, and I know there are other horizons beyond that."

"And you want to reach them all?" the *Marquis* asked.

"Of course!" Norina answered. "And you have brought me to the first one, but perhaps I will find the others only in my imagination."

The *Marquis* moved beside her. They stood in silence until Norina said:

"The newspapers have come, and I know you are longing to hear what is happening in England, so we had better go inside and I will read them to you."

She took him by the arm as she spoke and assisted him along the balcony. They passed through another window into the *Salon*.

It was a room she found exquisite, all in white with

French furniture, and pink curtains which were the colour of the geraniums outside.

She picked up the newspaper and read the head-lines, then the Editorial.

The *Marquis* appeared to be listening.

Yet when she asked what he would like read next, he hesitated. It was as if he had been listening to her voice rather than to what she said.

She read him a rather dull description of Queen Victoria's visit to Kew Gardens and an even duller speech made by the Prime Minister which had been severely criticised by the Opposition.

Then the door of the *Salon* opened and Jean came in.

He had in his hand a telegram.

"This has come from the Villa that is on the road above us, *Madame*," he said. "They regret it has been delayed, but they were away from home and the postman pushed it through the door."

"Is it for me?" Norina asked in surprise.

"Yes, *Madame*," Jean replied, "but the name of the Villa was incorrectly spelled and the Postman made a mistake."

Norina took it from him.

She looked at it and saw that not only was the name of the Villa mis-spelt, but so was the *Marquis*'s.

"Whom is it from?" the *Marquis* asked. "I thought no one knew you were here!"

It was then Norina guessed who had sent it and tore open the envelope.

For a moment the writing on the form seemed to swim before her eyes. Then she read:

127

*HIDE QUICK FROM MONK STOP SHE
KNOWS WHERE YOU ARE STOP—DAWES.*

She read it again, then gave a shrill cry of horror.

"What is it? What has happened?" the *Marquis*
asked.

"I have . . . to hide! They will . . . kill me!
Please . . . help me . . . where . . . can I . . . go?"

Norina got to her feet with the telegram in her hand.
Now she flung herself down on her knees beside the
Marquis's chair.

"My stepmother has . . . found out where I . . . am!
I have to . . . go away . . . at . . . once!"

"Your *stepmother*!" the *Marquis* repeated quietly.
"So it is she who has made you so frightened!"

"Sh-she tried to . . . kill me!" Norina said. "I . . .
I was only . . . saved because . . . I was not . . . hungry
and gave . . . my dinner to the . . . cat . . . and he . . .
d-died at . . . once!"

She gave a little gasp and cried:

"Now that . . . she knows . . . where I am . . . she
will . . . come here! She will . . . kill me . . . one way
or . . . another! Hide me . . . please . . . hide me . . . !"

She put out her hands, and the *Marquis* took them
in his.

The strength and pressure of his fingers was com-
forting.

"Suppose you start from the beginning," he said
quietly, "and tell me your secret and what all this is
about."

She would have moved away, but he held her
hands. She put her head down against his knee.

"My . . . stepmother," she murmured, "is . . .

wicked . . . evil . . . and she . . . wants my money . . .
the money my mother . . . left me . . . when she
d-died.''

"But your father is alive?''

"My father is . . . Lord Sedgewyn.''

"I have heard of him,'' the *Marquis* remarked. "I
believe he has some race-horses.''

"A few,'' Norina admitted, "but he prefers hunt-
ers, and was . . . very happy in the . . . country
when . . . my mother was . . . alive. Then . . . he married . . . again.''

"And you say your stepmother wants to kill you?''

"She thought my father was . . . very rich . . . but
then she discovered that . . . the money he spends . . .
is mine and it only . . . becomes really his if I . . . die
before him.''

"And she has actually attempted to kill you? I can
hardly believe it!''

"It is . . . true! It is . . . true! And I . . . ran
away . . . because I . . . knew no one would . . . believe
me . . . and if I told . . . any of my relatives . . . they
would . . . only say I was being . . . hysterical and . . .
laugh at me!''

"I believe you,'' the *Marquis* said.

"Then . . . please . . . help me! I do . . . not want
to . . . die! I want to live . . . and . . . and I have
been . . . so . . . so happy here.''

The *Marquis*'s fingers tightened on hers.

"You are not going to die,'' he said. "Do you
really think I would allow anyone to kill you?''

"But . . . how can you . . . prevent it? She will
put . . . poison in my food again . . . or she might
get . . . somebody to . . . shoot at me . . . while I am in

the . . . garden. There are a . . . thousand ways by . . . which I could lose . . . my life . . . and no one . . . would ever . . . guess that she had . . . murdered me!''

"Who told you this was what she intended?'' the *Marquis* enquired.

"It was Dawes. He is Papa's valet, and he has been with us ever since I was a baby . . . and he is the . . . only person I can . . . trust.''

"So it was he who sent you the telegram!''

"Yes, and it was Dawes who went to Hunt's Domestic Bureau in Mount Street to find me . . . somewhere to go, but they . . . said the only vacancy was . . . yours. That was . . . why I was so . . . frightened you would . . . refuse to . . . employ me.''

"But I have employed you,'' the *Marquis* said, "and now we have to make certain this wicked woman does not succeed in her desire to do away with you and gain your money.''

"Can we . . . do that? Where . . . can I . . . go?''

"It is quite easy,'' the *Marquis* replied.

"Easy?'' Norina asked.

"My yacht is in Nice Harbour. I sent for it as soon as I arrived.''

"Your yacht!'' Norina breathed. "That means we would be at sea and she could . . . not approach . . . me.''

"Not unless she can swim or fly!'' the *Marquis* answered.

Norina gave a sigh of utter relief and shut her eyes.

The *Marquis* put his hand on her hair.

"You will be quite safe,'' he said, "until I am well enough to contact your father or someone who will make sure that your stepmother never tries to kill you again!''

"I have . . . been . . . so afraid,'' Norina said.

"Of course you have,'' the *Marquis* answered. "And now that you have told me what has been frightening you, everything will be far easier.''

"You are . . . sure of . . . that? But . . . there is no . . . reason why . . . you should become . . . mixed up in this . . . horrible situation.''

"I think, Rina,'' the *Marquis* said, "we have been together long enough to know that we both have an obligation towards each other.''

"Now that I have . . . told you what is . . . frightening me . . . you will not . . . send me . . . away?''

"I will tell Jean now that we will join the yacht tomorrow morning. He will send somebody to alert the Captain, and we will be aboard before your stepmother or anybody else can be aware of it.''

"That will be . . . wonderful!'' Norina said. "And thank you . . . thank . . . you for . . . being so . . . kind to . . . me.''

The *Marquis* stroked her hair, and she felt as if the crimson light of the sun were moving through her.

It was such an unexpected relief to know that she was no longer alone in her fight against her stepmother.

The *Marquis* was beside her, defending her, helping her.

Quite suddenly, because there was no need for her to go on fighting, she felt limp and as if she might collapse.

"You are tired,'' the *Marquis* said quietly. "Go to bed now and sleep without dreaming. To-morrow we will leave here and return only when it is safe to do so.''

"How can I ever be safe?"

"I am not certain," the *Marquis* said quietly, "but somehow we will find a way."

"I will pray . . . I will pray very hard that you will do so," Norina said, "and when I say my prayers to-night, I will thank God because you are so under-standing."

The *Marquis*'s lips opened, and she thought he was about to say something.

Then as if he changed his mind, he said:

"Go to bed, Rina—if that is really your name."

"Actually, it is 'Norina,' " she said, "Norina Wyn. I called myself 'Wyndham' because it was easy to remember."

The *Marquis* laughed.

"You are always practical, even in a storm," he said. "One of the things I most enjoy about you is the way your brain works."

Norina looked at him.

Then, because she felt there was no other way to thank him, she bent forward and kissed his hand.

She rose to her feet.

"Good-night, *Monsieur*," she said, "and thank you . . . thank you!"

The *Marquis* did not answer. As she suddenly felt shy, she ran from the room.

Only as she went upstairs to the next floor did she think of a thousand ways in which she might have expressed her gratitude better.

'He understands . . . I am sure he . . . understands,' she thought.

She reached the top of the stairs.

She knew Jean had seen her leave the *Salon*, and now he would have gone to his Master to guide him to his room.

To make it easier while his eyes were bandaged, the *Marquis* slept in a bedroom on the same floor as the *Salon* and the Dining-Room.

It was not as impressive as his usual bedroom, which he had designed himself. This was on the same floor as the one occupied by Norina and had a fine view of the sea.

But as he could not see, it was not for the moment important.

What was important was that Jean's room was beside his in case he needed any attention during the night.

Norina went into her own room.

There were a number of servants in the Villa, but they had a separate house of their own.

It was at the back, so once they had retired, there was no noise to disturb the *Marquis* or anybody else.

'It is so peaceful,' Norina thought as she undressed.

How was it possible that her stepmother's evil hands could reach out to her? Therefore, she had to lie and pretend to be somebody other than herself?

She would be safe in the yacht with the *Marquis*.

If anybody knew she was alone with him and that she was her father's daughter, her reputation would be ruined for ever.

"What . . . does it . . . matter?" Norina asked.

At the same time, she knew it would distress her father, and also her mother if she were alive.

"There is . . . nothing else I . . . can do," she said,

''but how can this . . . go on for . . . ever?''

As she asked the question, she was afraid of the answer.

Because she wanted to sleep rather than to think, she got into bed.

She was just slipping away when suddenly something was placed over her mouth.

She awoke with a start.

Before she could realise it was not just a frightening dream, her mouth had been forced open and a gag tied tightly behind her head.

She could not utter a sound.

A rope then encircled her body, and something dark and heavy covered her completely.

She tried to struggle and attempted to scream, but it was useless.

Strong arms were carrying her from the bed.

Then she realised in horror that she was supported on ropes, and was being let down over the balcony outside her room to the floor below.

Her feet were bare and she could feel the night air on them.

What covered her face and most of her body made it almost impossible for her to breathe.

She knew only that she was being taken away on her stepmother's orders.

Long before the *Marquis* was even aware that she was no longer in the Villa she would have been killed.

Everything that was happening was done so precisely and so cleverly. The men, and she was sure there were a number of them, made not a sound.

As she reached the balcony below, two men lifted her in their arms. She knew they were carrying her down the flight of steps that led into the garden.

They were walking across the lawn to the end of the garden. There were rocks that ended in the sea.

She thought despairingly that the *Marquis* would not know where she had been taken. There was no way of telling him.

Then, as she struggled against the ropes that pinioned her arms to her sides, she was aware that she still wore her mother's wedding-ring.

Pushing her third finger with her thumb, she managed to loosen it.

Just at that moment the men came to a stop. She guessed they were above the rocks that led into the sea.

Although there was still very little sound, she could hear the lap of the waves. She guessed there must be a boat waiting.

She pushed the ring until it slipped from her finger.

Another moment and it would have been too late. The men moved forward and now she knew they were standing on the rocks. They passed her to two other men who were standing lower down.

Then she was handed over to two men who were in the boat.

She could feel it rocking beneath them, and they put her down in it.

The men involved in her kidnap climbed in and started to row.

The sea was calm as they moved swiftly and without speaking.

'I am lost . . . I am lost!' Norina thought. 'They will . . . throw me into the . . . sea and when I am . . . washed up on the . . . shore I will be . . . dead!'

She felt her whole body tense with fear as she waited for the moment when the men lifted her up. Perhaps they would remove the ropes before they pushed her into the water.

But the oarsmen rowed on and on. Suddenly there was the sound of the bow of the boat being embedded in sand.

She heard two men spring ashore and start to pull the boat farther from the water.

When they had done so, they were lifting Norina again.

Then she knew she was not going to die—at any rate—not by being drowned.

At the same time, she had no idea where she had been taken, and she could only cry in her heart:

"Save me . . . save me!"

She was praying to God, but it was a plea that also went out to the *Marquis*.

How would he know, how could he guess that she had been carried away in this frightening manner?

Where would he begin to look for her?

"Help me . . . oh . . . help me!" she cried.

Then she thought that perhaps because she loved him he would even, if he were asleep, hear her voice calling him.

She was picked up again.

Then one man spoke in French, saying to the other:

"We've done that job well! No one heard us, and Father Jacques'll be pleased!"

"That he will," another replied, "and if this one's anything like the last, we'll all get a good 'rake-off'!"

"Which is no more than we deserve!" the other man said.

Father Jacques!

That must be the Monk against whom Dawes had warned her.

How could she have been so stupid? With the telegram coming so late, she should have left the Villa to-night and not waited.

She should not have listened to the *Marquis*'s idea that they should join the yacht to-morrow.

'Dawes warned . . . me! He . . . warned me!' Norina thought miserably. 'Only I was too . . . foolish to . . . understand!'

Then she was praying again, sending up a cry that came from the very depths of her being to the *Marquis*.

'Save me . . . I love you! No one else will . . . hear me . . . save me! Save me!'

It came to her mind as she prayed and cried that she should have let him kiss her once as he had intended.

Then she would have something to remember as she died.

chapter seven

"BRING me a brandy and soda!" Lord Sedgewyn said as he finished his bath.

When Dawes had one waiting for him, he said:

"I am tired, Dawes."

"Yer're doin' too much, M'Lord!" Dawes replied.

"I know that," Lord Sedgewyn answered, "but I am also worried about Miss Norina. I wonder where she can be?"

Dawes did not answer.

He only helped his Master into his evening-coat.

He was thinking as he did so that His Lordship was much thinner and more lined than he had been even a few weeks earlier.

Lord Sedgewyn finished his brandy and walked towards the door.

"Do not wait up for me, Dawes," he said. "I do not expect to be back until the early hours."

Dawes watched him as he walked down the passage and thought to himself:

"She's killin' 'im, that's wot she's doin' with 'er parties and suchlike!''

He drew in his breath.

An idea had come to him, and he knew it was something he had to do.

He tidied the bedroom and waited until he knew Lord and Lady Sedgewyn would have left the house.

Then he walked down the corridor.

As he did so, Miss Jones, Her Ladyship's maid, came out of the bedroom almost bumping into Dawes in her hurry.

"Yer're in a rush!" Dawes said accusingly.

"I know," Miss Jones replied. "I'm goin' out, an' it's about time! Toodle-oo!"

She ran down the corridor as she spoke, and Dawes watched her until she was out of sight.

Then he went into Lady Sedgewyn's bedroom.

He locked the door behind him. He started to look for the key of the cabinet which was attached to the wall over her wash-hand-stand.

During the years he had been in service, Dawes had grown used to finding keys of safes, of despatch-boxes, of jewellery-cases, and a number of other things.

He located the key he wanted under the lining-paper in the centre drawer of the dressing-table.

Going to the small cupboard over the wash-stand, he found what he sought. It was behind some bottles, hair-tonics and throat-sprays.

It was a very small bottle, dark and rather sinister-looking.

Dawes was certain it was what he was seeking.

He pulled out the cork and sniffed it, and knew he was not mistaken.

Then he walked to the side of the bed, where he knew Miss Jones would have left Her Ladyship's *tisane*. She drank it every night to make her sleep.

It was a mixture of honey and herbs besides, Dawes suspected, a little luminal if she had been very late.

He poured into it a teaspoonful of the poison.

He was sure that was all that would be required, and he put the bottle back in the cupboard. He locked it and replaced the key from where he had taken it.

He walked down the corridor to have his supper.

He was thinking he had not only saved his Master to whom he was deeply devoted, but also Miss Norina.

* * *

Norina felt herself deposited roughly on what she thought was a bed.

Then the heavy material over her head was removed and for a moment she thought she had gone blind.

Then she realised the room into which she had been taken was in darkness.

She could not even see the men who were removing the ropes that were wound round her body and the ones that tied her ankles together.

She could only feel their hands touching her. She was too frightened even to breathe.

One of them pushed her head sideways and undid the gag that was knotted at the back.

It had hurt her mouth and her throat was dry. Although she wanted to scream, no sound would come.

Then a rough voice said in French:

"*Voilà!* You stay here quietly or we'll gag you up again. The Prior'll speak to you in the morning."

There was the sound of their footsteps walking on a bare floor towards the door.

Then, as it shut behind them, the key turned in the lock.

Norina was unable to move.

She could only lie stiff and terrified, thinking for the moment, at any rate, they had not killed her.

She was startled by a voice saying in English:

"Who are you? Do you speak English—or— *parlez-vous Français*?"

In a voice that did not sound like her own, Norina replied:

"I . . . I am English."

"Oh, good! Now I can talk to someone! But why did you come here?"

"I . . . I have been . . . kidnapped."

"That is what they did to me."

"Where are we?" Norina asked. "Please . . . tell me where we are."

"We are in the Convent of St. Francis, which is on a small island off the mainland, and I believe once the Monks who lived here were good and holy men, but now they are evil and wicked!"

"I . . . I think they are . . . going to . . . kill me!" Norina said, and now there was a break in her voice.

"They will do that later," the English girl answered.

"They . . . will? H-how do you . . . know?"

The girl lowered her voice as if she were afraid she might be overheard.

"Every girl who comes here or is kidnapped is rich,

and they make us sign documents handing over everything we possess to God and the Convent, which is really them!''

Norina made a little murmur.

Now she understood why Dawes had warned her against the Monk. It was her stepmother who had arranged for her to be brought here.

When they had killed her, her money would be Violet's.

"I suppose you are rich," the girl said.

"I have . . . some money," Norina admitted, "but my stepmother . . . wants it . . . all so I cannot quite . . . understand what will happen if I make it . . . over to . . . the Monks.''

"I expect she will give them half, or something like that," the girl said. "I know that is what will happen where I am concerned.''

"You have . . . signed away your . . . money?'' Norina asked.

"They made me sign the papers, as they will make you.''

"How will they do that?''

There was silence before the girl said:

"You will learn that to-morrow from the Prior, but I do not want to frighten you.''

"I . . . I would rather . . . know what to . . . expect," Norina said.

"They ask you to sign the documents, and if you refuse, they say you must do penance for your sins and they flog you!''

Norina gave a little cry.

"I do . . . not believe . . . it!''

"That is what they did to Imogen, who was another

English girl who was brought here. When finally she gave in and signed the papers, the next day she was drowned!''

Norina bit her lip so as not to scream.

She was afraid that if she did so, the men who had warned her not to make a noise would come back.

Now she could see the whole plot quite clearly. She knew that unless by some Miracle the *Marquis* could save her, she, too, would be drowned.

''How can they get away with this?'' she asked when she could speak. ''Surely somebody will be anxious about the disappearance of these girls?''

''If they are, they obviously do not complain,'' the girl answered, ''and my mother's lover, who has arranged that I shall die, will certainly celebrate my death by drinking more than he usually does!''

She spoke bitterly, but somehow calmly, which was more upsetting than if she had cried.

''Surely we can do something?'' Norina cried. ''I do not . . . want to . . . d-die.''

''Nor do I,'' the girl who was talking to her said. ''But the man who has arranged for me to be murdered is giving my mother drugs and, when the money has been shared out by the Monks, I am quite sure he will kill her too.''

Norina felt she could hardly believe what she was hearing.

Lying in the darkness, it was like living in some terrible nightmare from which she could not wake up.

''What is your name?'' the girl beside her asked.

''Norina. What is . . . yours?''

''Claire, and my father, when he was alive, was

144

Sir Richard Bredon. He was such a kind and wonderful man.''

''You can only . . . pray that your father will . . . help you now,'' Norina said, ''as I am . . . praying to my . . . mother.''

''Do you really think our prayers will be heard in a place that has been desecrated by thieves and murderers?''

Norina did not answer.

She was praying frantically, praying that she would not scream and draw attention to herself, praying that she might yet be . . . saved.

But only God would know how that was possible.

Claire did not speak to her any more, and Norina knew she had gone to sleep.

She herself dozed a little before she was awakened by the light showing through the rough curtains over a window.

Her first thought was that it might be a way of escape.

She jumped up to run to it, but when she looked out she knew why it was not barred as she might have expected.

There was a sheer drop down into the sea.

The waves were moving gently against the rocks on which the Convent had been built.

Only the most powerful swimmer, she thought, would be brave enough to dive into the sea not knowing how deep it was.

As she stood looking at the mist that hung over the sea, as the sun rose a voice behind her said:

''There is no escape that way.''

She turned and saw that Claire was sitting up in the bed next to hers.

Now she could see that the only furniture in the room were two iron bedsteads. The walls were of ancient stone without any covering.

Claire was a pretty girl with dark brown hair falling over her shoulders, small features, and long-fingered hands which she held out now to Norina.

"You are lovely!" she exclaimed. "Just as I thought you would be, and I am so glad you are here. It has been frightening with no one to talk to."

Norina went back to sit on her bed.

"Are there any other girls here?" she asked.

"Oh, yes," Claire answered. "There are nearly a dozen. Some of them are older than us, but we are the only ones who are English now that Imogen has gone."

"Are they all rich?"

"I suppose so," Claire said, "but I speak only a little French. There are some who speak Spanish and others who are Italian."

"And you really think the Monks intend to . . . drown them all?"

"They may have other ways of disposing of them," Claire replied, "but they certainly drowned Imogen, and I suppose . . . I am next!"

"Do not speak like that," Norina said quickly. "We have to escape, or perhaps if we pray hard enough, somebody I know . . . will come and . . . rescue us."

"The Monks never allow anybody to come onto the island," Claire said, "and I think they have guards at the front entrance to the Convent at night."

Norina's heart sank.

There was the sound of a key being turned in the lock.

As she was wearing only a thin nightgown, she got quickly back into bed.

A man dressed as a Monk, but with a hard, ugly, common face, looked round the door.

"Here's a robe for you," he said in French to Norina, throwing it down on the floor, "an' you're both to come down to breakfast immediately."

He spoke the words in French in a surly tone. Then he pulled the door to again and they heard his footsteps walking away.

Norina got out of bed.

"Did you understand what he said?" she asked Claire.

"I understood *petit déjeuner*," Claire replied, "and in a moment or two we will hear the bell. If we do not hurry, there will be nothing left to eat."

Norina was putting on the robe, which she realised was that worn by a postulant Nun.

It was of a very coarse material and, she thought, none too clean.

There was, however, no use complaining and Claire, who had got out of bed, was putting on her clothes.

They consisted of a few underclothes in which she must have arrived at the Convent, then a robe which was similar to the one the Monk had brought Norina.

Somewhere in the distance there was the loud clang of a bell, and Claire said:

"Hurry, or the other girls will eat everything!"

She ran off as she spoke. Norina followed her down

some twisting, uncarpeted stairs, then along a narrow corridor.

She had a quick glimpse through a window of a statue surrounded by cloisters on each side.

They reached a long low room in which there was a refectory table, where a number of young women were hurrying to sit down.

On the table there were three loaves of bread and a small amount of butter.

There was also a large pot of what smelt like cheap and unpleasant coffee and a number of cups without saucers.

The girls and women, who were a miscellaneous collection, were all grabbing at the loaves of bread. They were pulling rather than slicing pieces of them.

They seemed to Norina like animals.

Then she realised they were hungry. Like animals, they had to fight for every crumb to assuage their hunger.

She made no effort to compete, but Claire snatched a piece of bread and divided it.

"Here you are," she said. "It will have to last you until luncheontime. Let us go and get a cup of coffee while we have the chance."

Norina took the bread, and as she was about to put it into her mouth, she asked in a whisper:

"You do not think it is poisoned?"

"No, no, they will not kill you until you have signed the documents," Claire answered.

It was cold comfort, and Norina ate the bread.

Then she managed with Claire's assistance to obtain a quarter of a cup of coffee which was all that was left.

As she was looking at the girls, wondering if she should speak to those who were French, a man dressed as a Monk came to her side.

"Come with me," he said curtly in French. "The Prior wants to see you."

Norina gave a frightened glance at Claire, but she knew she had to obey the order.

The man walked ahead, his heavy shoes clattering on the stone floor.

As she followed him, Norina could see that the Convent had once been a fine building and was undoubtedly ancient.

It was now, however, very dilapidated.

Stones had fallen from the walls, and the square which was surrounded by cloisters was thick with weeds around a statue of St. Francis.

It was obvious that nothing was being done to preserve the place or even keep it tidy.

The man ahead of her stopped and opened a door.

As Norina walked into the Prior's room, she could see that he, at any rate, lived in comfort.

There were deep armchairs, a fine writing-desk, pictures on the walls, and heavy, rich velvet curtains at the windows.

The Prior was waiting for her with his back to a medieval fireplace.

He looked, Norina thought, exactly as she might have expected.

He was a large, portly man, and what hair he had, which was very little, was grey.

She thought she would have recognised him anywhere as being a criminal.

His eyes were shrewd and his lips were set in a hard line.

She could feel every instinct in her body shrinking from any contact with him.

The man who had brought her there did not speak, but merely withdrew, shutting the door behind him.

Norina stood looking at the Prior.

"Good-morning, Norina!" he said, speaking in good English. "Welcome to our Convent! I know you are waiting to discover why you are here."

"I have some idea of that already," Norina replied.

"That makes things easier," the Prior answered. "I have some documents for you to sign on my desk, and I expect you have already been told the penalty for disobeying my orders."

Norina felt a little tremor of terror run through her, but she lifted her head proudly.

"I can hardly believe," she replied, "that as you pretend to be a Man of God you would really do anything so appalling, so unmerciful and wicked!"

The Prior laughed, and it was a very unpleasant sound.

"As you knew before you ran away, your stepmother requires your money, and, of course, this Convent is a very expensive place to keep up."

Norina did not answer, and he said in a jeering tone:

"Come along, my dear, give up your worldly goods to God, and you will, of course, get your reward in Heaven!"

He looked towards the desk as he spoke. Norina saw on it were some official-looking papers.

She knew he would force her to sign them.

If she did so, she reasoned, then undoubtedly she would die as quickly as it could be arranged. Then he would not have the expense of keeping her.

Somehow she knew she had to play for time.

Then, almost as if a voice, and perhaps it was her mother's, prompted her, she gave a little groan and collapsed slowly onto the floor.

Her eyes were closed, and she lay there motionless.

The Prior swore and they were French words that Norina had never heard before, but she knew they were lewd.

Then he went to the door and shouted:

"Henri! Gustave!"

Two men came running into the room.

"She has collapsed or fainted," the Prior said in a tone of disgust.

"Shall we slap her back into consciousness?" one of them asked.

"No, take her away," the Prior said. "Put her in her room and give her no food. She will be amenable enough when she is hungry!"

The two men lifted Norina from the floor, and she forced herself to be completely limp.

She kept her eyes closed and hardly breathed as they carried her back the way she had come, along the passages and up the staircase which led to the room she had slept in the previous night.

They threw her down on the bed rather roughly. Yet she managed not to make a sound.

She merely lay where she had been thrown, one arm hanging over the side of the bed.

"We'd better lock her in," one of the men said. "That's what the Prior said."

"What about the other English girl?"

"Oh, she'll have to sleep somewhere else. There's plenty of beds available for them as can pay for them!"

The other man laughed as they went out of the room and locked the door.

Norina waited until she was quite certain they had gone. Then she went to the window.

If only there were someone to whom she could signal!

If she could wave, they might realise she needed help.

But there was only the Madonna-blue of the sea, which, now that the sun had risen, reflected the sky overhead.

Once again she knew there was nothing she could do but pray.

*　　*　　*

The day passed very slowly.

As it grew dark and no one came near her, Norina wished that Claire were with her. At least she would have somebody to talk to. She was also growing hungry.

'I suppose I shall have to sign the papers,' she thought desperately.

Darkness came and the stars filled the sky. There was a moon, not full but a half-moon, which turned the sea to a silver enchantment.

Norina lay on her bed.

She had taken off her robe because she felt it was

unclean. Fortunately it was not a cold night, and there was no wind.

She was praying, at the same time thinking of the *Marquis* and how much she loved him.

'He will never . . . know when I am . . . dead that I have . . . given him my . . . heart,' she thought.

She was so carried away by her thoughts that she did not at first hear a faint sound at the door.

It was now too dark to see clearly, but she thought it opened. She was instantly afraid, but in a different way from before.

Supposing one of those rough men had come not to kill her, but for a very different reason?

Because she was so frightened, she could only lie still. She was filled with a sudden terror because somebody was in the room, and coming slowly towards her.

Their feet made no sound, but she knew they were there.

They reached the bed. Then, when she would have opened her mouth to scream, her lips were captive and two strong arms enfolded her.

She felt a sudden rapture streak through her whole body.

It was the sensation she had felt when he touched her before, and she knew who it was.

Then the *Marquis* said very, very softly so that she could hardly hear:

"Do not make a sound. You have to be very brave."

She wanted to tell him she loved him. Instead, she could only put out her hands to touch him and make sure he was really there.

He lifted her off the bed, and to her astonishment took her to the window.

She wanted to tell him there was no possible escape that way.

Then she realised he was putting a rope round her which in some strange way was attached to him.

Yet she could only think he was beside her. Nothing else in the world mattered.

The rope had come not from inside the room but through the window. Before she could wonder how, the *Marquis* said:

"Now you have to be brave. Shut your eyes and hold on to me. I promise you you will not be hurt."

She looked up at him, and for the first time saw in the faint light of the moon that his eyes were unbandaged.

"You . . . can . . . see!" she whispered.

He put his fingers on her lips, and she felt ashamed that she had spoken.

Then he put one leg out of the window. Because she was tied to him, she was obliged to do the same.

"Shut your eyes," he whispered again.

She felt a pull on the ropes he had attached to her as they were lifted over the sill.

She knew a moment's panic as she realised they were swinging in air, at the same time being lowered into the sea below.

Then the *Marquis*'s arms enfolded her and she could hide her face against his shoulder. She told herself if she died now, she would die with him.

They were lowered slowly, clear of the rocks. At last two men were holding first their feet, then their bodies, and guiding them into a boat.

It was quite large, and the men removed the rope by which they had descended.

Then the boat was moving away. Norina found herself sitting in the stern with the *Marquis*'s arms round her.

He did not speak, but they were rowed very swiftly out to sea.

It was a little later that Norina saw the *Marquis*'s yacht looming up above them.

She was helped aboard, and as the *Marquis* joined her he took her through a door and inside what she guessed was the Saloon.

There were no lights anywhere. Norina knew it was because everything had been done in secret so that they would not be seen.

Then, as the Saloon door closed behind them, she was in the *Marquis*'s arms.

"You have . . . saved . . . me," she whispered, "you have . . . saved me . . . how . . . can you have . . . done so? I thought . . . I was . . . going to . . . d-die."

It was then, because she could not help herself, that she burst into tears.

The *Marquis* picked her up in his arms and sat down on a sofa. He held her across his knees as if she were a child.

"It is all right, my darling," he said gently, "you are safe and this shall never happen to you again."

It was the way he spoke as much as the endearment which made Norina forget her tears. She raised her face to his.

"H-how you . . . could have . . . come . . . like an Archangel from . . . Heaven . . . and taken me . . . away from that . . . e-evil place?"

Her words were almost incoherent.

At the same time, she was looking up at him as if he were in fact not human, but a Messenger from God.

"I had to save you," the *Marquis* answered, "not only because I could not let you die, but because you are too precious to lose, and I love you!"

As he finished speaking, his lips found hers.

He kissed her until she thought she must, in fact, have died and reached Heaven.

His love swept over her like a wave of the sea.

Yet there were stars in her breast and the light of the moon, or perhaps it was the Light of God which dazzled her eyes.

The *Marquis* kissed her until they were both breathless.

Then she said in a little voice he could hardly hear:

"I . . . love you . . . but I never . . . thought . . . you would . . . love me!"

"I have loved you for a very long time," the *Marquis* replied, "but I wanted to see you with my eyes as well as with my heart before I told you so."

"And now . . . you have . . . saved me!"

Norina realised that as they had been talking, the engines had started up and the yacht was moving.

"You have . . . saved me!" she said again. "But there is another . . . English girl . . . there and a lot of . . . others. How can we . . . save them?"

"It is all arranged," the *Marquis* replied. "The Police are moving in at dawn and three *gendarmes* are already on the roof. They let us down. Because I would not have you involved in all that cruelty and wickedness, I persuaded them to let me get you away so that you will not have to appear at the Inquiry."

"H-how . . . can you . . . have been so . . . clever?" Norina asked.

"I was thinking about you, my darling," the *Marquis* said, "and also, of course, of—myself. Do not forget that we are both in hiding."

She put her hand to his face.

"Your bandage has . . . gone and you are . . . just as I thought . . . very, very . . . handsome!"

"I have to wear glasses in the daytime," the *Marquis* replied, "but not for very much longer."

His lips were very near to hers as he said:

"I would be prepared to become completely blind rather than allow anyone to rescue you except myself!"

His arms tightened.

"I was so desperately afraid there would be a mistake at the last moment, or that I would not be in time."

"H-how . . . did you . . . know . . . how did you . . . guess where I had gone?"

"I found your ring," the *Marquis* replied. "It was clever of you, my precious, to leave it for me, and I also knew what had been in your telegram."

"And you . . . thought the Monk from . . . whom I was warned to hide . . . must have come from the . . . island?"

"The Police have been suspicious for some time of the men who have taken over the ruined Convent, but, as no one had made any complaint, there was nothing they could do."

"And you gave them the excuse they needed to enter it."

"*You* did that," the *Marquis* replied, "but I will not have you having to face all that unpleasantness, so we are going away, my darling, on a very long honeymoon."

Norina gave a little cry.

"How can...you think of...anything so...wonderful? But...please...are...you quite... quite certain that you...want to m-marry me?"

"I am certain," he said, "because I can fulfil what you demanded!"

His lips moved against the softness of her cheek as he said:

"I love you with my mind, my heart, and my soul— and also, my precious, with my body, and of course, my 'Inner Eye.'"

"That is...how I...love you," Norina whispered.

The *Marquis* did not answer.

He was kissing her again, kissing her until she felt little flames rising within her to answer the fire on his lips.

Then she was aware, a little belatedly, that she was wearing only her nightgown.

She made a little murmur and hid her face against his neck.

Her heart was beating tumultuously, and she could feel his doing the same.

"You must go to bed," the *Marquis* said, "and now that we are away from the island we can put on the lights, but I feel it will make you shy to be seen as you are now."

Norina slipped off his knees. He put his arm round

her to help her to the door and down the companion-way.

He took her to the end of the passage and opened a door of what she was sure was the Master cabin. It was so large it filled the whole of the bow.

"I must . . . not take . . . this cabin . . . it is yours," Norina said quickly.

"To-morrow night it will be *ours*," the *Marquis* answered. "We are being married, my darling, on French soil, and because I am a Frenchman, there will be no difficulties. After that we can go anywhere in the world you like."

"Anywhere . . . will be . . . Heaven if I am . . . with you," Norina answered.

He put his arms around her. Then, instead of kissing her passionately as she expected he was going to do, his lips were very gentle.

"I love and adore you," he said, "but I know, my sweet, that you are very innocent, and I have no wish to shock you."

He lifted her into the big bed and pulled the covers over her.

Norina caught hold of his hand.

"Promise me that . . . I am not . . . dreaming," she pleaded, "and I will . . . wake up to find I am . . . still a . . . prisoner."

"You are my prisoner now," the *Marquis* answered, "mine—from now until eternity—and I will never, and this is a vow, my Love, lose you or let you go."

"That is . . . what I . . . want to . . . be," Norina said, "but . . . will . . . you promise me . . . something?"

"What is it?"

He sat down on the edge of the bed and bent towards her.

"I am so afraid . . . that I will . . . bore you," she murmured, "like . . . those other . . . ladies who . . . write to you."

The *Marquis* would have spoken, but she went on:

"Will you . . . teach me how to . . . keep you happy and content so . . . that I do not . . . lose you?"

He could hardly hear the words, but he smiled.

"You have already told me how to do that," he answered.

She looked up at him in surprise.

"Have you forgotten," he asked, "my Château in the country and how you said I ought to settle down and produce a large family?"

Norina made a little murmur. His arms were round her as once again his lips were very near to hers.

"I have a great deal to teach you," he said, "and it will be the most exciting thing I have ever done in my whole life! You are mine, my lovely Norina, as I am yours, and nothing will ever divide us."

He gave a deep sigh before he said:

"I suppose all my life I have been searching for love—the real love that you understand—and now, my precious, we have both found it, and this is where the real adventure of life begins—our life together!"

Then his lips were on hers, and Norina knew that he was right.

They had found the only thing that mattered; what all men sought, fought for, and died to find.

It was the love of the mind, the heart, and the soul, when two bodies were joined together as one.

They had passed through dangers, wickedness, and evil, yet by the mercy of God they had survived.

"I love you, *Mon Dieu*, how much I love you," the *Marquis* exclaimed.

And then there was only LOVE and more LOVE going on to Eternity.

ABOUT THE AUTHOR

Barbara Cartland, the world's most famous romantic novelist, who is also an historian, playwright, lecturer, political speaker and television personality, has now written over 507 books and sold over 500 million copies all over the world.

She has also had many historical works published and has written four autobiographies as well as the biographies of her mother and that of her brother, Ronald Cartland, who was the first Member of Parliament to be killed in the last war. This book has a preface by Sir Winston Churchill and has just been republished with an introduction by Sir Arthur Bryant.

Love at the Helm, a novel written with the help and inspiration of the late Earl Mountbatten of Burma, Great Uncle of His Royal Highness The Prince of Wales, is being sold for the Mountbatten Memorial Trust.

She has broken the world record for the last sixteen years by writing an average of twenty-three books a year. In the *Guinness Book of Records* she is listed as the world's top-selling author.

Miss Cartland in 1978 sang an Album of Love Songs with the Royal Philharmonic Orchestra.

In private life Barbara Cartland, who is a Dame of the Order of St. John of Jerusalem, Chairman of the St. John Council in Hertfordshire and Deputy President of the St. John Ambulance Brigade, has fought for better conditions and salaries for Midwives and Nurses.

She championed the cause for the Elderly in 1956 invoking a Government Enquiry into the "Housing Conditions of Old People."

In 1962 she had the Law of England changed so that Local Authorities had to provide camps for their own Gypsies. This has meant that since then thousands and thousands of Gypsy children have been able to go to School, which they had never been able to do in the past, as their caravans were moved every twenty-four hours by the Police.

There are now fourteen camps in Hertfordshire and Barbara Cartland has her own Romany Gypsy Camp called Barbaraville by the Gypsies.

Her designs "Decorating with Love" were sold all over the U.S.A. and the National Home Fashions League made her, in 1981, "Woman of Achievement."

She is unique in that she was one and two in the Dalton list of Best Sellers, and one week had four books in the top twenty.

Barbara Cartland's book *Getting Older, Growing Younger* has been published in Great Britain and the U.S.A. and her fifth cookery book, *The Romance of*

Food, is now being used by the House of Commons.

In 1984 she received at Kennedy Airport America's Bishop Wright Air Industry Award for her contribution to the development of aviation. In 1931 she and two R.A.F. Officers thought of, and carried, the first aeroplane-towed glider airmail.

During the War she was Chief Lady Welfare Officer in Bedfordshire looking after 20,000 Service men and women. She thought of having a pool of Wedding Dresses at the War Office so a Service Bride could hire a gown for the day.

She bought 1,000 gowns without coupons for the A.T.S., the W.A.A.F's and the W.R.E.N.S. In 1945 Barbara Cartland received the Certificate of Merit from Eastern Command.

In 1964 Barbara Cartland founded the National Association for Health of which she is the President, as a front for all the Health Stores and for any product made as alternative medicine.

This is now a £650,000 turnover a year, with one third going in export.

In January 1988 she received *La Médaille de Vermeil de la Ville de Paris*. This is the highest award to be given in France by the City of Paris for achievement—25 million books sold in France.

In March 1988 Barbara Cartland was asked by the Indian Government to open their Health Resort outside Delhi. This is almost the largest Health Resort in the world.

Barbara Cartland was received with great enthusiasm by her fans, who fêted her at a reception in the City, and she received the gift of an embossed plate from the Government.